BABY GIRL

lenora adams

simon pulse
new york   london   toronto   sydney

This book is a work of fiction. Any references to historical
events, real people, or real locales are used fictitiously. Other
names, characters, places, and incidents are the product of the author's
imagination, and any resemblance to actual events or locales or
persons, living or dead, is entirely coincidental.

SIMON PULSE
An imprint of Simon & Schuster Children's Publishing Division
1230 Avenue of the Americas, New York, NY 10020
Copyright © 2007 by Lenora Adams
All rights reserved, including the right of reproduction
in whole or in part in any form.
SIMON PULSE and colophon are registered trademarks
of Simon & Schuster, Inc.
Designed by Tom Daly
The text of this book was set in Galliard BT.
Manufactured in the United States of America
First Simon Pulse edition February 2007
2 4 6 8 10 9 7 5 3 1
Library of Congress Control Number 2006920464
ISBN-13: 978-1-4169-2512-5
ISBN-10: 1-4169-2512-0

This book is dedicated to Gloria Nyutu-Blackman,
Laura Dixon-Hartshorn, and Lucille Maiden.
"Thank you!"

PLANTING
SEASON

Dear Moms,

I know you're probably wondering where I am and why I left. The first question is easy—I'm still in Pennsylvania, but several miles away in a small town called Lancaster. I am staying at a place called Milagro House, which is kind of like a long-term shelter for teenage girls and women, but please don't come here. Right now I need my space. I'm just letting you know that I'm okay so you won't worry.

I'm sure what you really want to know is why. Why am I here? "Why" is the same question everyone here at Milagro House is asking me too. All I can say is that I never thought it would come to this. I never thought I would run away. For some reason I thought you of all people would see and know—know as soon as the seed sprouted. Know what's going on and perhaps help me

3

understand it too, because something gnawing inside of me tells me that the real answer is buried in my story. Our story.

Here at Milagro House I have lots of time to think, so I've been thinking about my life, and what I realize is that this was my destiny. All these years I had fooled myself into thinking you could rescue me, but you hadn't saved yourself yet. Perhaps as I write this letter we'll both figure out the deeper reason why—why my path is so similar to yours, why I didn't learn lessons from the past. So to help me and you learn, I have to start at the beginning of the summer, because that set off my chain of events.

"Damn! Of all places, why here and why now?" I grumbled as I threw my head and hands up to the dark sky. On such a clear hot night not a moonbeam or star could be seen, but the sky was the only place I wanted to look. I couldn't bear to look at my girl. Her car was torn up!

Yet Ange's tears weren't for the stolen CDs, money, or Louis Vuitton makeup bag, or even for the slashed tire. All of that stuff, including the black 2002 Honda Civic, was replaceable. The tears were for the trouble that, thanks to some vandals, was surely coming.

We weren't supposed to be in this part of Philly.

Three months ago, when Ange's dad, Mr. Rinaldi, gave her the car, he ordered her not to drive it to Philadelphia. Ironically, his concern wasn't because she was a newly licensed driver, and even Dale Earnhardt Jr. could have trouble maneuvering on the Schuylkill. No, Mr. Rinaldi didn't want his "princess" in Philly. No parts of Philadelphia!

After tears and screams of "I hate you," Ange and her mom, Isabella, eventually wore Mr. Rinaldi down. He gave a little, allowing her to drive to South Philly. Her nana and practically all of Ange's aunts, uncles, and cousins lived in the southern end of the city. They were some of the last people to stay in the old Italian neighborhood. Working-class Italians used to live in most of the homes in that section. Today, some might call it a melting pot: blacks, Irish, Latinos, and everyone else who dared to cross the invisible boundary lines making the old Italian neighborhood their home too.

Ange never said why her relatives stayed in the city, refusing to move to the burbs like so many others had done. No, they kept their roots planted. So whether someone was an original or a transplant, they recognized the Rinaldi name. It carried weight. I suppose that's why Mr. Rinaldi gave Ange permission to travel freely there. He thought she'd be safe.

But there we were in Point Breeze! At the wrong

place and at the wrong time. Ange's junior license had expired over an hour before.

Usually, when Ange and I got in a jam, her brother, Tony, or her mom helped us out. But Tony had stayed at college to take extra classes. In the summer? When it's nice outside? Like, ninety degrees? Shut in a classroom? I don't think so! From what I heard, Tony had trouble just walking his muscular legs to classes during the regular school year. He was a serious partyer, and I was sure that's how Tony was really spending his vacation at State College. Four and a half hours away, Tony couldn't help us on this night.

Isabella? She'd often been Ange's partner in crime. But this was a mechanical type of thing. Ange's mom certainly wasn't any good with these types of late-night problems. In fact, Isabella's a better schemer than cleaner-upper. We can tell her what we're going to do before we do it. But if you-know-what hits the fan, like in the present situation, she's not the one to call.

There were no more choices. Reluctantly, I looked over at Ange. There was no need for words. She understood it was time to bite the bullet.

Tossing her long, thick, wavy hair aside, she pulled out her cell phone, opened it, and said "home." Within seconds, Ange was shrieking like a newborn in her daddy's ears.

"Dah-dee, you got to come help me! Someone broke into my car and they slashed my tire. [She sobbed.] I'm not really sure where I'm at and I'm scared."

Sometimes Ange could make even Pinocchio proud. She knew where we were. Since the beginning of May we had been coming to Point Breeze, hangin' with Raheem and his boys. Raheem and Ange were messin' around. But lookin' at her car windshield, where someone had scribbled with burgundy lipstick "Stay away white bitch!" somebody had a problem with that. I said to myself that we would deal with that somebody later. At that point, I was more concerned about dealing with Mr. Rinaldi.

Although I couldn't hear what Mr. Rinaldi was saying on the phone, I could tell by Ange's answers that he couldn't understand how she didn't know where she was.

Through fake tears, Ange said, "Dah-dee, wait, okay? Sheree asked someone to tell us what part of Philly we're in and what street. We're on Greenwich Street in the twenty-two-hundred block in . . . [She turned to me and winked.] What part of Philly did you say, Sheree?"

Catching on, I loudly answered, "Point Breeze."

"Okay, did you hear that, Dah-dee? How long will it take you? Yeah, we'll be all right. We'll go back to our friend's house and wait until we see your car. Okay. Bye, Dah-dee."

In an instant, she clicked off the phone, wiped her drying tears, laughed, and said, "C'mon. We just bought ourselves some more time."

Before high-fiving Ange, I needed to know the story. 'Cause you know, Moms, I'm not used to lying. Not that I'm tryin' to front. 'Cause yeah, I've lied before. Still lie to teachers about leaving my homework or books at home. Doesn't everybody? But I don't lie to you. You, Stacey Renee Jemison, don't play that! I've learned that you only play it with yourself and with your man of the moment.

As far back as I can remember, you repeatedly warned me, "Don't lie to me, Sheree. I hate liars and I hate sneaky people too." When I was a kid, the penalty for lyin' was a beatin'. Now I suspect you don't have the energy for all that, 'cause now you threaten to throw me out of the house. And I know you ain't playin', either. If you caught me in a lie, you would straight-up kick me out. So I don't lie to you; there's no point.

Besides, you made it so there's nothing I can't tell you and nothing you can't tell me. You know where I go and who I'm goin' with. So I suppose you better than anyone understand my need to know the "story" before Mr. Rinaldi arrived.

After Ange dropped the details, we went back inside Raheem's house. A few hours earlier, the place had been packed with his friends from the neighborhood and his old college, filling spaces in the tiny row house. But when we returned, only Raheem and his three boys remained, along with two girls. They were all sitting in the tiny, faded green kitchen smokin' an' rollin' blunts. Hovering over the weed was jasmine incense, Raheem's favorite scent. He often lit it to disguise the joint smell from his mom, Ms. Jordan, who would be home in the morning. Ms. Jordan is a tall thick woman with graying hair and a sweet voice. She works the night shift at Tastykake. Although Ange and I didn't see her too much, we often helped ourselves to the products she helped bake.

Standing in the kitchen, watching Raheem and his friends, I couldn't tell who the girls were on. But Russell, whose name everybody pronounces Rah-sool, was feelin' this dark-skinned chick. She looked a'ight, a little too skinny, though.

The girls were friendly enough, but I got the feeling they weren't happy to see us. Ange, who doesn't always read people's faces or expressions well, was clueless.

"Somebody messed up my car!" she shared with the partyers.

Unsuccessfully trying to mask their pleasure, the two girls snickered. But it was brief and my annoyance was reserved for Ange. I don't know why she had to

9

broadcast it to everyone. She had already told Raheem about the car when he answered the door. That's all that needed to know. I didn't want these girls in our business! I just didn't trust something about them.

"Whoever did it is just jealous," I added while eyeing the mocha girl with the ponytail weave.

"Yo, that's messed up!" Russell said as he passed Ange a joint. "Here, take a hit."

As Ange carelessly reached for the joint, I grabbed her arm and pulled it away. "Your dad will be here soon. You don't want him to smell weed on you," I whispered in her ear.

Totally disregarding my warning, Ange put the j to her lips and took two hits. Tapping my arm, she attempted to pass it to me. I looked at her like she was loco. Mr. Rinaldi wasn't smelling weed on me! My gut told me he didn't even like me, so I wasn't giving him any ammunition.

Raheem took what would have been my hit and the joint worked its way back around the table.

About an hour later, we spotted a tow truck and Mr. Rinaldi's large white Mercedes Benz.

"Ange, your eyes are so red! You know I don't have Visine," I said as we ran toward the car.

"Angela, get in the car! You too!" Mr. Rinaldi's deep voice cut through the darkness. Give or take a few inches, Mr. Rinaldi is about five seven, five eight—a good four or five inches taller than me, but still kind of short for a man. However, something about his deep Italian voice makes him seem much bigger. He also has a way of raising his thick eyebrows that makes me nervous. It's like he can see my thoughts or something.

While Mr. Rinaldi and the tow truck operator examined Ange's car, she and I got into his. When her dad returned, we tried to act like we were asleep. Just as I suspected, Mr. Rinaldi wasn't fooled. He started the car and said, "Angela Isabelle Rinaldi! What were you doing down here? Didn't I tell you South Philly only? It's dangerous down here! Anything could have happened to you! And you don't even know where you are? Why were you here? You should have been home hours ago! Did you see what was written on your windshield? They must know you! *Disgrazia!* Who is it? How come they have problems with you? What did you do? It must be a warning. . . . Well? Answer me!"

Answer which question first? I don't get it. Adults do this all the time. Ask questions they really don't want an answer to. This was one of those instances. Ange didn't even open her mouth and pretend like she was about to answer. She just kept staring at him. When it seemed like he was done, she grinned. Yeah, grinned! Not a big-mouth, teeth-baring grin, but a gentle, *It's okay, how are you?* type of grin. It was weird. If I gave you a look like that, you probably would have slapped the Juicy Fruit taste out of my mouth. Mr. Rinaldi didn't even seem to notice.

Instead, he continued talking. "Ange, you are not to come down here again. Do I make myself clear, young lady?"

This time an answer was expected.

"Yes, Dah-dee."

And that was it. End of discussion. Just like on TV. How come we don't fight like that? Ange settled back into her same position, head against the passenger window, and I remembered to breathe again. As soon as Mr. Rinaldi pulled into our neighborhood, I started playing my wishing game. I wished no one would be hangin' out on the corner. I wished the houses were bigger, farther apart, and surrounded by more grass. I wished there wasn't any trash on the street or sidewalks. I wished my neighborhood looked more like Ange's.

Obviously, my wishing didn't change things one iota. It didn't even wipe out the look of disgust Mr. Rinaldi had on his face as he glanced at our house. I know this man doesn't like me, or where I come from. By the way, I happen to like our tiny flower garden.

"Thanks, Mr. Rinaldi. Good night, Ange. Talk to you tomorrow."

Mr. Rinaldi drove off as I was still fidgeting with the locks. He didn't even wait to see that I got into the house.

Before I shut the front door, I checked for your keys. They were in their usual spot on the front room table. Since Regal's was still open, I was surprised you were already home. You would normally still be perched on the first bar stool. That was your spot. You could see everybody who came in and they could see you, too.

After all these years, I still haven't figured out why it's even called Regal's. The darkness, the musty smell, the stained wooden floor, the ripped watermelon-colored bar stools, the plastic glasses—nothing about the place or the people who go there is regal. Of course it took me a while to figure that part out. When I was a little girl, I thought the place was da bomb. I used to love it when you took me there. I'd sit at the bar stool right next to you, watching your every move. You'd have a Tanqueray and ginger ale. I'd have a Shirley Temple. Leon, the short, pudgy bartender, always gave me two cherries.

He'd wink at you, and say in his raspy voice, "Here, sweetheart. Remember, don't give your cherry to the first person you meet." Then you and he would laugh. The message was over my head.

Even still, I'd sit there, feelin' like a big girl on those bar stools. Every time you took a sip, I would too. Just as if I was watchin' the Smurfs on TV, my eyes were glued to the way the men talked to and touched you. Some would be real nice to me. Buying me barbecued potato chips. Another Shirley Temple. A fish sandwich. Or give me money. You'd often say, "Take that money, Ree Ree." Dutifully, I'd grab it and give the person a kiss on the cheek. Proudly, you'd smile at me, probably thinking, *That's my girl!* Before I could even check to see the year near George Washington or Abraham Lincoln's face, you'd grab it. Tucking it in your bra, you'd say, "Got to put this in your piggy bank when we get home."

You knew I didn't have a bank.

The money man would talk to me for a few more seconds, asking me the usual questions, most of which had been answered before: age, grade in school, favorite subject, be when I grow up. Feeling like they made a connection with me, they'd move on to you, slipping under your spell.

You know how every little girl thinks her moms is the prettiest? Well, that's what I thought about you. Still do. I remember how you used to always wear your black catsuit. Remember? You'd wear the skintight black zip-up spandex suit, with riding boots and a black riding hat. The zipper would be pulled just so it covered south of the border. Depending on how you moved, anyone could catch a glimpse of the side of your breast. I especially loved how you would cock your hat to the side and look like you were goin' to your next riding lesson. Everybody knew there weren't any horses in our part of town.

That was one of my favorite outfits. And the guys at Regal's? Even the married ones loved it too! I could tell by all of the looks and stares you got when you wore it. The men's eyes would follow you around, like a mother duck leading her ducklings. And the women? They often whispered or rolled their eyes. "Ree Ree, women are just jealous like that," you'd tell me.

It was on one of those days, sitting at the bar and watching how men were captivated by you, that I decided I wanted to be just like you. I wanted to dress like you. I wanted to sound like you. I wanted to look like you. I wanted men to look at me with begging eyes, the way they did you. I wanted to be like you so bad that I took to copying you.

At home I often practiced how you smoked. I'd take out a Newport that I stole fresh from your purse, pretend to look around for the right person to light it. Once I caught his eye, I'd give him a soft half smile, showing more lips than teeth. When it was lit, I'd inhale, then I would tap my pretend airbrushed nails on the bar, in this case the kitchen table, and slowly blow the smoke out of my slightly upturned, partially closed lips.

But that was back in the day. A child's game. I've since outgrown tryin' to be like you. Heck, I inherited your body. So now I don't want to be like anybody but me, whoever I am.

On that night, after Ange's car situation in Point Breeze, I was getting tired, so I went upstairs. Your door was shut. Stealthily, I placed my hand on the knob and carefully tried to twist it. It was locked. I wondered who you had in there.

Knowing not to bother you when you had company, I went to my own bedroom, where I locked my door. Nothing is worse than having some drunken or highed-up fool "accidentally" walkin' into my bedroom. Remember how one of your friends used to do that?

That old cat named Marcellus used to walk in all of the time. Between you and me, I know he did it on purpose. He would try to catch me just as I got out of the bathtub and was in my room. Or he'd just walk into the bathroom while I was peein'. He'd pretend like he didn't know a shut door meant someone was in there. He was quick. But I was quicker! As soon as I would hear my doorknob rattle, I'd cover up or wake up. I could be dead sleep, hear that sound, and be fully alert. I'd always say the same thing loudly: "Mr. Marcellus, Moms's room is the next door." He'd apologize. Act like he forgot. But c'mon, I'm not stupid! I had a poster of Lil' Kim on my door. What twenty-seven-year-old did he know that had posters on their door?

Yeah, there was somethin' about that Marcellus I just didn't trust. Thank God you didn't keep him around too long. Every once in a while, mostly when you were broke, you'd get back with him. Oh, how I hated when money was tight. Marcellus had a job at the post office sorting mail or something like that. You always bragged about how it was a good job with good benefits. As a kid I'd think it couldn't be that good or he'd be outside delivering it. Moms, I used to try real hard to get you to forget about him. But when the bills were deep and money was hard to come by, you always banked on Marcellus. The fool was always open.

Even though I didn't like Marcellus, I never feared him. I just didn't feel comfortable around him, that's all. I also couldn't see what you saw in him, with his big belly and stinky feet. Remember how you used to make him leave his shoes on the stoop? You didn't want the funk in our house. What did you see in him? It had to be the money, 'cause you've done better.

Your next boyfriend, Dayday, was cute. Out of all of

them, I liked him the best. It wasn't just because he put locks on all of the doors. He was cool, too. But the locks? Yeah, that was the move, right there! Just by pushing a little knob in, I was finally able to sleep uninterrupted each night. And I was able to lock the bathroom door too. No more keeping my guard up. I finally had privacy.

I wished I'd had it long before. Several years ago, before there were locks on the doors, before Marcellus, before Mom Mom moved out, one of your boyfriends . . . I'm sure you know who I'm talkin' about . . . Kevin?

When I first met him, I thought he was cute too. I thought y'all were gonna get married. Remember how he used to take me everywhere? And you know how adults always say, "When we get inside this store, don't ask for nothing"? Kevin never did that. He'd always ask what I wanted, and he'd buy it too. He didn't care that I already had a Cabbage Patch Kids doll; he'd buy me another one. He didn't seem to worry about cavities, either. I could buy and eat all the Mary Janes I wanted.

When Kevin was around, we were like a family. We did things like most families do. We went to the movies and out to dinner, took pictures at the mall together, and went to Chuck E. Cheese. You name it, we did it. I can honestly say you loved him and it wasn't about payin' bills. Yeah, he had some cheese, but you and he were for real.

However, Mom Mom wasn't feelin' Kevin. From jump, she told you she didn't like him. "Stacey, there's something about him that ain't quite right. I can't put my finger on it, but I feel it in my bones," Mom Mom often said.

I was ten years old, in the fourth grade. Although my breasts were blooming faster than most teenagers were, and my butt was getting plumper, I was much too young to understand the wisdom in Mom Mom's words. Perhaps, at twenty-five, you were old enough to heed Mom Mom's warning. Maybe you should have checked him out a little bit better, taken off those rose-colored glasses. But in all fairness, you saw what he showed you. A man who loved you, who happened to love and care for your daughter, too. "A rare find"— that's what you told your girlfriends he was.

Kevin talked about doing this thing right. Getting a bigger place for the three of us. Getting married. Being a real family. So you fiercely defended him against Mom Mom's verbal attacks.

As time wore on, war was taking place between you and Mom Mom. Y'all began creating space with each other, as I did too with Kevin. Going out for ice cream, or to the movies, no longer appealed to me. I wanted to be left alone. But you kept pushing us together, forcing the family thing. Why?

You usually seemed to know what was on my mind. You were good at busting me for stealing your cigarettes. Or for not coming straight home after school. Or for stealing from the corner store. Why were you blind this time? Couldn't you see?

When Kevin came over, I no longer ran into the room and fell into his open arms.

"Sheree, that's no way to say hi. Give Kevin a hug and a kiss," you'd say to me.

If he asked me to sit on his lap, I'd remind you that I was ten years old.

"Girl, you ain't grown. I still sit in Kevin's lap. You used to love sitting in his lap." You'd badger me some more.

The more I pulled, the more you shoved. Until finally, you were forced to see, to see my truth. . . .

It was on Saturday, cleaning day. I was upstairs changing into another shirt when Kevin silently walked into my room. I turned around, saw him, and froze. *No, not again,* I thought! We'd been here before. He no longer had to play the tickle game, or find the dollar, or any of his stupid games. I just wanted it to be fast and over with so I turned back around and waited. I prayed to God, *Please don't make him make me touch his ding-*

a-ling, don't let him jam his tongue into my mouth.

From behind, he roughly grabbed my right tittie. Then my left . . . and squeezed. He was making them almost touch. My eyes fixed themselves on the poster of the group Immature, which was hanging over my bed. As Kevin dropped to his knees, his large calloused hands began rubbing on the dots on my titties. The lead singer, Marques Houston, was staring back at me. Kevin pulled me closer. It's strange, but instead of paying attention to Kevin, I remember thinking, *I want to marry Marques.* Then Kevin made some type of sound. I did too.

The sound of my own voice confused me. I bore into Marques's eyes, begging. In my mind I hated what Kevin was doing. But my body? My body was just flustered. My blood was racing. And . . . and . . . my coochie felt . . . *my coochie felt!* My coochie didn't used to feel. It was a coochie. It was for peein'. When Kevin touched me, my coochie felt hot. And my panties? They started stickin' to me. I thought I had peed my pants.

Kevin kept rubbing my titties and breathing real hard.

"Aah . . . you are so beautiful."

In my mind I ordered Marques to look away!

Just as Kevin was fumbling with the button on my shorts . . . I turned back to God in prayer, *Please don't let him put his fingers in my coochie . . .* and then *you* saved me. However, I didn't want you to see me like that.

The expression on your face quickly changed from shock to rage. I've heard you cuss a thousand times, but not as angrily as you did that day. You bombarded Kevin with a slew of curse words. You slapped and punched him. Tried to kick him in his ding-a-ling.

"Why? Why?" you begged between each blow.

His answer, and your response, blew me away.

"She . . . she . . . she started rubbing all up on me, Stacey. She even grabbed my johnson."

No longer spellbound by Marques Houston, wide-eyed, I watched you and Kevin and wondered, *What's a johnson?*

The tears came when you slapped me across the face, snapping my head back. "You need to stop bein' so fresh. Your damn body's growing like wildflowers! Keep it covered!"

Wildflowers! A nice enough name, but a curse word in our house. Why must all of our relatives use plants and flowers to describe things? Nothing is ever just yellow or blue. A great aunt may say, "Her kitchen is the color of a beautiful coreopsis." Or they may use it to describe an attitude. "Chil', why you have blue stars?" instead of simply askin', "Why are you feelin' down?"

Once I overheard Mom Mom talking to you in the kitchen, warning you that if you didn't bring me up

22

better, I'd be like a wildflower. At the time, I didn't understand Mom Mom's meaning. But as I got older and began helping her prune her flower beds, the subtle message grew on me. Wildflowers can be hard to control. Despite the environment, water, and soil quality, the flowers can take on a life of their own, growing freely. Perhaps that's why Mom Mom, her mother, and her mother's mother were all container gardeners. Although by nature they had green thumbs, to them there was something unnatural about seeing a field of blossoms. No, they preferred their flowers to be carefully surrounded by mulch and other types of bedding, always growing under their control.

I had hoped speaking in flowers would have skipped your generation, but there you were standing in my bedroom, calling me one. After yelling at me and slamming my door, I listened as you kicked Kevin out of the house. I waited for you to come back upstairs, tell me what I needed to hear.

Four words.

I waited.

Ears still glued to the rhythm of your walk, I heard you come back upstairs and slam your bedroom door shut. It was my fault? My eyes couldn't avoid Marques Houston's any longer as I was begging for forgiveness that even he couldn't give to me.

Hours later, when my tears were dry and the Immature poster ripped to shreds, you opened my door. The four words? Today, I'm still waiting.

At ten years old, I didn't understand why we couldn't tell Mom Mom about it. Why we couldn't even tell Roc. Why was I told to forget about it?

A few days have passed since I started this letter. Bringing up the past isn't easy, but it's necessary, to get to my truth and to help explain why I am in this situation.

Despite Mr. Rinaldi's warning, once again Point Breeze was calling Ange's name. She hadn't seen Raheem since the night of the car incident. So she was itching to see her man. You know me—always itching to leave Ardmore, so I was along for the ride. Wearing a jean miniskirt and tube top, I was lookin' good.

"Oh, shoot! I gotta go back home. I forgot my phone."

We hadn't reached the expressway when Ange hung a U-ie toward her home. We pulled into the large driveway and Ange clicked open the garage door. Each time I returned from Ange's house, you always asked for a description, wanting to know what was inside these rich people's mansions in Lower Merion. A simple enough curiosity.

The old three-story traditional home made of stone had large double windows, window boxes full of colorful flowers that you and Mom Mom would have loved. There was also a small balcony, two front doors, a stone patio, and a swimming pool.

As nice as the outside of the house was, it didn't compare to what was inside. All of the furniture was dark and heavy-looking. I know that sounds ugly, but as I told you before, actually it was very beautiful. It looked like it had been there before, timeworn, but not at all hand-me-downish. Or museum-type, either. Thanks to Eleanor, the housekeeper, the Rinaldi house was clean. It was also well lived in. No one put anything away. Eleanor did it all.

My two favorite rooms were Ange's bedroom, with her large off-white canopy bed, and the dining room. The dining room was painted with faded golds, reds, browns, and orange. Something about the dining room warmed me. It was also the only room in the entire house that celebrated the family's Italian ancestry.

Anyway, the house looked pretty much the same when Ange and I entered. Her mom's car was in the garage, so we knew Isabella was somewhere around the house. It was much too early for Mr. Rinaldi to be home.

As we cut through the family room, we surprised Isabella and one of her girlfriends. The two women quickly threw a newspaper over the small mirror on the oval coffee table. If they had moved a millisecond faster, my eyes wouldn't have caught the powder or the razor.

Agitated, Isabella questioned, "Angela, you're back so soon?" She self-consciously wiped her nose. "I thought you were going to see Raheem? How long are you two staying here? Hi, Sheree."

The look on Isabella's face told us she didn't like being surprised. We were invading her space. The tone of her voice was quickly moving us out the door. Eyes looking wild, Isabella's girlfriend didn't say a word. She, too, looked as though we were standing around five seconds too long.

After the explanation and retrieval of the cell phone, we were back on the road. Once again Ange was out of Isabella's way and, as usual, I was out of yours.

In the car Ange began fiddling with the radio stations. Every number on the dial was bangin', but she cruised the buttons anyway. Obviously fed up with the music, Ange huffed while turning off the radio. She then began twirling her hair around one finger. Seconds later she was pushing the radio back on and cruising the stations again. I recognized the signs. She was tryin' to quiet her mind. Tryin' to digest . . . erase Isabella's not-so-well-hidden secret. Ange wasn't fooled. She's known all along what her mom and her friends are into. Still, knowing doesn't mean accepting. I chose to silently ride out Ange's sudden burst of hyperactivity. We'd talked about this before. No new words would, could, change who our parents were.

By the time we got to Raheem's house, Ange's mind seemed to do whatever it normally does with unwanted information. She was back. As we pulled up, Raheem's mom, Ms. Jordan, was pulling off, heading to work—something Raheem didn't know anything about.

When we went inside, Raheem and Russell were already firing one up. Ms. Jordan probably hadn't even driven around the corner yet. While I began mellowing out, escaping my own problems, Ange's high took her in another direction. She was horny. Obviously horny. Horny to the point where she was even making me uncomfortable. Carrying her away, as though she were a bride, Raheem handled his bidness. Russell and I watched videos. Swizz Beats, Timbaland . . . their beats were bumpin' against the noise upstairs. When Ange and Raheem emerged sweaty and funky from the bedroom, I teased, "Y'all are so loud!"

Ange blushed.

Smiling like he won Powerball, Raheem asked, "Who's hungry? Let's go to Friday's. Angela, you got me, baby?"

I like Raheem and all, but that brotha be poor. He

27

never has any money. Never. He's never so much as bought Ange a soda. Yet for someone who has empty pockets, his gear is tight. He's got, like, four different pairs of Timberlands and two throwback jerseys. Ange didn't give him all of that. But she's given him enough. I keep schoolin' Ange, tellin' her to stop diggin' in her pocketbook. But she just laughs at me, saying, "It's only money. It's no big deal."

As I write this, I can hear your voice screaming about men and money, so yes, I told Ange it *was* a big deal, that he was maybe juicin' her. But Ange didn't care. She looked at it as only her daddy's money. She never had to work. Didn't know what a chore was. Allowance was just given, never withheld. Plus, she got a platinum credit card in her and Mr. Rinaldi's name. If she ran short, there was always more money on the way. So, for her, it was just money. Why would she value it?

So naturally, Ange would cover Raheem at the restaurant. After she freshened up in the bathroom, we headed to the Friday's on City Line Avenue, the four of us piled in the Honda. When we all go someplace, Raheem almost always takes over the wheel. Acting like it's his car. Flipping radio stations. Readjusting the seat. And driving fast. He claims to have a license, although I never saw it.

At Friday's we lucked out and got seated right away.

Ange was all over Raheem. For the record, Russell and me are cool. We ain't feelin' each other. So there's no need to sniff around. I think he likes 'em taller and skinnier anyway. That ain't me with my short bootylicious self. Although Russell is cute, he's only got a little bit more in his pocket than Raheem. Clearly not my type!

After eating and chillin' for, like, three hours, it was time to bounce. Ange wanted to get home early. So after dropping Raheem and Russell at their houses, we hit the Schuylkill. It wasn't eight o'clock yet, but Ange was racing to beat Mr. Rinaldi home. She figured it was still too soon after the last car fiasco to rock the boat.

"Ange, you're really feelin' Raheem, aren't you?"

She giggled. "Yeah, he's so cute. Tall, dark, and beautiful. Don't tell him I told you, but he says he's falling for me."

"Falling? . . . In love?" I coughed.

"Yeah! Don't laugh, Sheree. I know how you are about that stuff. I told him I already love him."

"Did you ask him when he's gonna get a job?"

Raheem is twenty years old, out of high school, without a job, which means no money. He doesn't even regularly sell street medicine. Every now and again he sells some weed, but that's it. He's not makin' any real paper. He doesn't even have his own car. Ange's Honda is his chariot. What Raheem has goin' for him is that he's fine. I'll give Ange that. He puts the *F* in "fine." *But he's broke!* Empty pockets never beat fine. Ain't that right?

Since the end of our junior year, Ange and me have been hangin' tough. During that time, I've noticed something about her. She falls in love frequently. Quickly. And hard! That in itself is bad enough, but then she always goes for the brothas, like Raheem, that ain't got nothin'. Yeah, the brothas are black and fine. She doesn't do ugly. But she does broke very well.

When Ange and I first started kickin' it, she confided in me, explaining to me her love of the dark meat. "I like black guys! I like the way their skin feels. I love their lips and the way they kiss. I love how they talk to me, taking control. I love all of that, Sheree."

Although I don't think Mr. Rinaldi is prejudiced—after all, they have a black housekeeper—he just doesn't approve of his "princess's" black boyfriends. I haven't met any white ones, so who knows if he'd trip over them, too. On the other hand, Isabella doesn't seem to mind. She lets Ange do whatever she wants. They keep Ange's dating activities on the DL from Mr. Rinaldi.

In school, people are always askin' me why Ange likes black guys. Like I'm gonna drop my girl's bidness? Instead I just laugh at their insecurity, flip it, and ask them what they want to know for. That usually shuts them right up. Some of the girls are just jealous. 'Cause you know, Ange is pretty with her dark, long wavy hair, olive skin, slender build, and pretty teeth. But for real, these girls need to relax. Ange isn't like me. She won't sweat anybody else's man.

Ange was clinging to her own man. I'm sure she was still thinkin' about love and Raheem when she pulled into our neighborhood. It was still early; she'd probably be home before Mr. Rinaldi. But the night was just beginning for me. On a hot summer night I knew the courts would be hoppin', so I had Ange drop me off there.

Surrounding the basketball courts, little girls on swings, tryin' to flip over; little boys on the monkey bars testing their strength, some playin' tag, others in the sandbox; young girls, over made-up and over-dressed, standing in the wings hoping to catch the attention of some teenage boys; old heads sitting on benches, reminiscing about their own long-gone days; and anybody and everybody else who had nothing to do. They were all at the courts. An excitement that only the summer can bring was hanging in the night air. I took it all in, then my eyes scanned. The grassy area by center court? Nope. To the left near the tennis courts? Nope. There he is, by the gate, standing off to the right. Leaning against a tree, lookin' cool on this swel-tering night, chillin' with his boyees. My eyes spied

Damon. I found him. But I wasn't moving in his direction. Not yet, anyway. Instead, I walked over to Danita and Annacelis. They were the only girls there I liked enough to talk to.

We talked for a minute about track, the summer, stuff like that. Although I'm cool with Danita and Annacelis, they're just acquaintances. I don't get deep into their bidness. They stay out of mine. We eat lunch together, run track together, and that's about it. You've never met them 'cause I don't bring them home. We don't swing together.

Although both girls are cool, they're not exactly my cup of tea, as Mom Mom often says. The only reason Annacelis is at the courts is because her man, Juan, is playing ball. If he weren't here, she wouldn't be. She follows him around, doing most of what he says. Last summer a few girls tried schoolin' her about lettin' him boss her like that, but she's "too in love" to listen. So you can see why my time spent with Annacelis is on a limited basis.

Danita is Annacelis's best friend. They've been tight since, like, the third grade or somethin'. If you see Juan, then you see Annacelis, and then you see Danita. A third wheel to some, Danita has never had a man of her own. It's not because she's ugly, either. Her chubby face is cute. I think guys would like her more, though, if she didn't talk so much. She's one of those girls who always has something to say about somebody. But since she pretty much keeps my name and my doings out of her mouth, I tolerate her.

Besides, you know my crew, Moms. Me. Myself. And I. It's easier that way. No jealousy, no competition. My business stays mine. After me, Jemina, Tammy, and them fell out, I didn't trust any other girls. Well, that is until me and Ange became tight. She's a part of my crew—if two people can be a crew. Ange is different from most of the girls around here. She's not a hater. She could care less that my boobs are bigger than hers are, or that some guys try to get with me. She doesn't try to compete, so I don't. She let's me be me.

When me and Ange started hangin', our classmates were surprised. Everyone always wanted to know why I hung with her. And you know people were askin' her even more questions about me.

You even asked me what was up. I remember giving you some generic answer that people hang out with people like themselves. By the look on your face, I could tell you didn't know what I was talkin' about. Your eyes told me you wanted to know more, but you never asked. So I never volunteered. Once again, I thought you might eventually see.

I thought you of all people wouldn't look with your

eyes. 'Cause that's what my classmates only use. They see the obvious differences: our contrasting skin color, our height, our economic backgrounds. But read on, Moms, read on. . . .

After chatting with Danita and Annacelis, I eventually worked my way over to my Chocolate Thunder. Damon. My man. You've never heard me call him my boyfriend. He's too old to be called that. He doesn't call me girlfriend, either—sometimes shorty, but mostly baby girl. I love it when he calls me that. He knows it too. Somethin' about the way Damon says it in his deep voice, drawing out the *l* in girl, that makes me feel so good inside.

"What's up, Damon?" I asked while tryin' to find his eyes behind his dark shades.

"You, baby girl." He lightly smiled.

"Me?" I cracked my gum.

I knew what he wanted and he had me. Just like that, we were walking to the crib. So much for the excitement at the courts. I was on my way. There would be no more conversation. His message was understood.

I knew you were probably at Regal's, so Damon and I would have the place to ourselves. Obviously, we played house. When we were done, I made him a sandwich. Grilled cheese with bacon. His favorite. Just the

34

way he likes it with lots of butter and five pieces of bacon. As usual, my cooking skills weren't enough to hold his attention. He ate it and got up to leave. Putting some sexiness in my tone, I asked him to stay and watch some TV.

"I promised Bird I'd catch up with him," he said.

Damon was always catchin' up with his boyees.

When I was a kid, you used to tell me to stop pokin' my lips out. You said I wouldn't get anything that way. You were wrong!

I poked my lips out as far as they could go and crossed my arms. Damon knew what I wanted.

"Sheree, look, I'm sorry." He uncrossed my arms, trying to hug me. "I gotta catch up with Bird. I'll call you later tonight. Look, here's some money. It's all I got right now."

A small smile crept across my face. The four Andrew Jackson's were better than nothin'. After he left, I tried to find something to watch. Nothing good was on TV, so I picked up the phone and found myself calling Austin.

Austin Stewart III is—well, was—a junior at Lower Harriton. He'll be a senior with me this year. Last fall he and his family moved to our area, although I hear they live in some big house in Bala Cynwyd. A lot of girls have been trippin' over Austin Stewart, including me, which is crazy. I mean, he's not my type. For one thing, he's young, just turned seventeen, the same age as me. He has his license, but not a ride of his own.

Secondly, despite his cornrows, there's nothing about him that's gangsta . . . pimped out or even thuggish. With such a pretentious name as Austin Stewart III, I suppose it's impossible to be anything but clean/straight/legit, although he does have some street in him.

That little bit of attitude must be outweighing the negatives, because there's something about Austin— something that makes me want him. Problem is, he doesn't want me. At least he acts like he doesn't. I think he is the first guy who hasn't fallen for my lines or into my . . . Perhaps that's why I have been tryin' to holla at him. You know, find out what he's really about. Whatever the reason, on that night I was bored and he was at home.

"Hey, Austin. You know who this is?"

"Yeah. What's poppin', Sheree?" He sounded pleased to hear from me.

"Nothing much. How come you weren't at the courts tonight?"

"I couldn't get the car and I wasn't riding a bike. Who was runnin'?"

"You mean who wasn't? It was packed. Besides, I didn't stay long. Me and Damon left."

"You're still with that old head? I thought you were leaving him alone."

"Austin, he isn't an old head," I whined. "Besides, why do you care if I'm with him or not?"

"It's not about me caring. It's about you always calling me up and complaining about him. I told you before, he's using you. I thought at least you'd follow my advice since you always call me with so many questions."

At that point I was asking myself why I called him. Sometimes I love Austin to death. He's cool and can be really nice. Other times, like this, I just want to strangle him! He can be annoyingly blunt. He acts like things are just so simple. I can't just walk away . . . away from Damon. Maybe if Austin came into the picture and gave me something to walk toward, maybe then I'd leave. But for now, I ain't got nowhere to go.

Needless to say, when Austin's in one of his "say whatever is on his mind" moods, our conversations don't last long. This one was no exception. Once again I found myself staring at the tan-colored walls in the living room. It was too early to call it a night. Unfortunately, it was much too late for anyone other than the corner boys to be hangin' out. I needed some company, someone to talk to. My first thought was to go out and chill with them for a bit. But then I thought of Damon. He'd cold flip if he caught me givin' his boys some time. So I decided I'd better stay put. Instead, I hit Damon on his cell. First punching star-six-seven. Although he says he doesn't, I know Damon sometimes ignores my calls.

Sweetly I said, "Hey, baby. What are you doin'?"

"Sheree?" I heard that rise in his voice that told me this wasn't going to go well. "I told you me and Bird got bidness to take care of," he explained.

I whined, "Well, how long is it gonna take?" He couldn't see my lips. "Don't you wanna see me again tonight? I know you're not too tired. You promised, Boo."

No longer hiding his annoyance, he gruffly answered, "Look, Sheree, it's gonna be a while! Don't sweat me. I'm busy right now."

"I'm not sweatin' you. I just thought . . . I thought you were comin' by, that's all. We didn't even get a chance to spend no real time together."

If this were anybody but Damon, they'd be listening to the dial tone. But I've never been that bold with him. He's not the type to play with like that.

He still hadn't said anything. He was giving me the silent treatment. If he were standing in front of me, he'd give me the icy stare, too. Even though we were talking on the phone, I was sure that he was probably cracking his neck, thinking of some lie to feed me. I broke the silence. "Where are you, anyway? . . . I know I didn't. . . . Who's that chick that just asked you who you were talkin' to? Damon . . . Damon! Can you hear me?"

Suddenly, I was the one listening to dead air. Switching the phone off, I waited a few seconds. Nothing. Quickly clicking the talk button on, I hit redial. No ring. Straight to voice mail. Oh, Damon will swear me up and down that his battery died. But I know the deal. I've been knowin' it. I just don't know why I'm still here.

As I was walking upstairs to bed, you walked in the house—you and one of your friends. Rodney. I never saw him before. After some quick introductions, I learned that he's from Chester. What was he doin' in Ardmore? His last name was never given. Since both of you were lit, I wondered if either of you knew the other's last name. By then, I knew the drill, having witnessed it so many times before. I continued walking up the stairs, into my room, and locked the door.

It was early Saturday afternoon before our house came alive. Peeking through the tiny holes in my shade, the bright summer sunshine woke me up, demanding my attention. Your nose awakened you from slumber. Bacon frying in the pan brought you and Rodney into the kitchen.

"Mmmm, Ree Ree, what else are you cooking for us?" you asked as you playfully hugged me from the back while I was flipping bacon.

How I desperately wanted to answer your question honestly. Nothing. But I knew you wouldn't be havin' that. So swallowing my sigh and keeping my eyes in check, I put more slices into the frying pan.

From the corner of my eye, I watched you and Rodney. There was a sort of distance. I don't know if I can describe it. But it was like y'all were seein' each other for the first time. I caught y'all stealing looks while the other wasn't payin' attention. He'd look you over. Like, *Um, she looks good for having a teenager.* You'd casually check him out. Like, *Okay, he's not bad lookin'.* Y'all didn't even really talk that much. As far as adult conversations go, y'all didn't say anything that my ears found interesting.

When I said the food was done, I noticed a slight hesitation. Should you fix his plate? Should he fix his own? I cooked; I was hardly serving. Rodney got up and got his own. He was quick, learning how it works. But then he got a little too comfortable! Taking his food to the front room, grabbing the remote, and changing the channel to ESPN.

After his belly was full, your man of the moment rolled out.

"Oh, Ree Ree, Rodney's got bank." You swooned as soon as the door shut.

I immediately recognized that light sound in your voice, and I knew what was coming. Spare me the details! I didn't care where he worked. Didn't care how much he made. Especially didn't want to know whether or not he was good in bed. I didn't care. Moms, I never did care about any of that. To avoid your juicy tidbits, I slipped on my Old Navy flip-flops and rolled out too.

Ange and I were supposed to meet up later to go shopping. But first I had to walk up to the Pike to get my nails done.

"Hey, Sheree."

A voice from out of nowhere startled me. Turning around, I identified the owner. "Oh, what's up, Greg? Where you goin'? Where's your boy at?"

"Who? Jerome?"

"Yeah. You know who I'm talkin' about. He's got his nose all broke into Lettica's—"

"Hey!" Greg stopped walking. "Hey, I ain't tryin' to hear all that noise. Why you always asking about them anyway? You still on him?"

No. I told Greg I wasn't likin' his boy no more. I just wanted to know what Jerome was up to. Plus, I'm still surprised he and Lettica Morgan got together. See, Moms, Jerome ran a game on Lettica and me. I know you taught me better than that, but somehow I got caught up. It happened in the beginning of eleventh grade. At first this gamer right here didn't recognize the hand.

See, Jerome Graham is different from the rest of these guys around here. He's actually smart. One day he's gonna leave this town and it won't be in a coffin or to rehab or prison. I can just tell he's one of those brothas that's gonna go far. Got a real future. Gonna roll in money.

And that's why I didn't recognize his attempts to be a playa. By all accounts he isn't one. Back then I was really feelin' him. I thought that if someone like him liked me, then I had a chance—a chance of breakin' out of Ardmore, a chance of bein' somebody.

But I was on a one-way street. Isn't that what you call it, Moms? Isn't that what you call love? Yeah, I was the only one with feelings. Jerome, like so many before, was about one thing. Oh, he didn't get it from me. Since I thought he was different, I was handling him different. Making him wait. I noticed schoolboys like him can wait awhile. While I was stalling him out, he caused me to give that girl Lettica I told you about some grief.

See, he was hollerin' at Lettica the whole time I was talkin' to him. But he twisted it. Isn't that what boys do? Had me believin' that she was always in his face, when everybody was knowin' he was in mine. Now you know, Moms, I wasn't havin' that! Ready to throw down, I stepped to Lettica. I was about to break her up too, but a teacher broke us apart. Neither of us got suspended—that's why you're just hearing about it now—but we had to go through something they call peer mediation. Translation: talk about our beef in front of some classmates. Through Lettica, I learned the truth about Jerome. It hurt. Showed me that even the so-called good guys got dog in them too. I felt bad because of how I treated Lettica. We made up and all, but we'll probably never be like Ange and me. That argument and almost fight will always be lingering under the surface.

Plus, Lettica's not the type of girl I'd really hang with anyway. We're like night and day. She's all into school, doesn't drink or smoke, probably still a virgin. Although Lettica is black, she sounds like a white girl, whiter than Ange. But for real, though, Lettica's a'ight. What I can't figure out is why she gave Jerome another chance. They hooked up at the end of my junior year. Once a dog, always a dog, but Lettica seems too smart to want to deal with fleas. I was hoping she'd leave him alone like I do.

* * *

When I got home from the nail salon, a wonderful smell greeted me at the screen door. Sitting at the kitchen table, you and Candy, enjoying. I joined y'all. I sat and patiently waited. Patiently because if I appeared too eager then you'd deny me. So I sat quietly. After two rounds, you nodded and the ganja made its way over to me. While the three of us smoked, the details I thought I had escaped poured out.

"Candy, Rodney had me climbin' the walls last night. He was that good, girl," you bragged.

Candy took a hit. "Um. I wish Todd could just get me on the wall." Candy laughed, and inhaled some more. "I'll climb it my damn self."

Teasing, you said, "That's because Todd is getting old and getting some from somewhere else."

"See, now why'd you have to go there? You're messin' with my high, Stacey."

Playfully rolling your eyes, you said, "Girl, you know and everybody around here knows he's creepin' with Marsha. You don't usually care, so don't get all siddity now."

"I know that's right! Todd can think he's creepin', but I'm the one holdin' the ace. Sheeit, he'd lose his damn mind if he knew Kyle was up in here too." Satisfied, Candy laughed some more.

"See, Ree Ree, baby? You've got to have one to pay

the bills. And one who makes you forget about the bills. Ain't no room for love in this game. Love is a dangerous game with no winners. And, Ree Ree, you gots to keep taking those pills! Ain't no room for babies in this game either. Ain't that right, Candy?" Visibly high, Candy shook her head. Standing on your soapbox, you continued, "Besides, Ree Ree, Moms here ain't old enough, ugly enough, or ready enough to be a grand-mom. If I become one too soon, you've got to go."

At least a thousand times! I think that's how often you've told me you'll kick me out if I become pregnant. I've got it. That's one of the reasons I'm here.

We were still smokin' when Ange knocked on the screen door. You knew she got on too, so you offered her a hit. Naturally, Ange accepted. The only person Ange had to hide from was Mr. Rinaldi. Isabella knew Ange smoked weed, but she wouldn't let her smoke it in the house. It must be due to the smell, 'cause Isabella cold busted us smokin' in Ange's car before, and she didn't say anything.

Once I told Ange about how you caught me and some girls from the neighborhood smoking. It was back when I was eleven. Do you remember that?

We were just smoking cigarettes, thinkin' we were cute. Also thinkin' we were hiding as we stood behind Mrs. Reed's garage.

Coming from out of nowhere, you surprised us, catchin' me with a cigarette hanging from my mouth.

Jemina stuttered, "M-M-Miss Stacey, hi."

Lookin' all scared, Tammy pressed her body into the brick garage, tryin' to camouflage herself. She was hoping you wouldn't see her or tell her mama. I was just hoping my beatin' wouldn't happen on the street. I didn't want my friends to see me, tough-talkin' Sheree, cry. You must have heard my prayer, 'cause you didn't even trip.

"C'mon, Sheree, time for you to get home," you ordered.

Throwing the cigarette to the ground, I gave my friends a parting glance. A look of doom. Tammy and Jemina fired the same look back at me.

While we were walking home you said, "Ree Ree, you're still young now, but when you're really ready to smoke, bring your cigarettes to me."

Tryin' to understand this new approach of yours, I stared. You didn't say anything more. There was no beatin'.

Three years later, me and my own pack of Newports sat in front of you. I no longer had to sneak. What was the rule? As long as I could buy my own, I could smoke in the house without any problems from you. Bumming cigarettes wasn't allowed. To celebrate my comin' up, a

46

shotgun. My first. Our first time together. Sitting in the kitchen smokin,' you laid out another set of rules. "Ree Ree, I want you to know what real bud taste like. If it doesn't smell or taste like this right here, then put it down, leave it alone, because something else is in it."

Rolling. Before, me and my friends always tried to steal blunts. We mostly got roaches or the occasional blunt, but never a bag of weed. Blunts were already packaged, so me and my friends never had to roll. We didn't know how, anyway. It was an art. Something you were actually quite good at. Eager to learn, I became your pupil. Carefully, I watched as you lined up the weed. Keeping it straight. Delicately licking and rolling the paper. So thin. So neat. Tighter than a Virginia Slim.

From that moment on, my life changed. I didn't have to douse myself with perfume before coming home anymore. Stolen roaches were no longer appealing. I could get and enjoy the whole thing. We could sit together. Smoke and chill. There would be no more stealing. No more secrets. And yes, like a good parent, you did warn me. "Ree Ree, I only smoke bud, weed, ganja . . . call it whatever you want. But that's all I mess with. I don't mess with anything else. No caine, no pills, no acid. Weed is all. That's all I will allow you to do. Stay away from that other stuff. You hear me? You know who the people are around here that's on the pipe. You see how messed up their lives are; let that be a lesson. Don't even think you can fool with that stuff just once. Can't nobody do that. Somebody comes at you with anything but killer, leave them alone. Don't even try to be grown and play. That other stuff is no joke. I'm serious now, you hear me, Ree Ree?"

Three years later, that smoking lesson was still ingrained in my brain. Cigarettes and weed, that was enough for me. After you, Ange, Candy, and I smoked a little, we parted ways. You and Candy, half-price night at Regal's. Ange and I, shopping at Suburban Square.

"I want a new bathing suit," Ange said as she looked through the racks of clothing.

The girl has at least ten bathing suits already. All of 'em two-pieces, still in style, and really cute. But at the moment, that's what Ange is into, bathing suits, cover-ups, and hats.

My obsessions haven't changed. Ever since that guy Bilal I was seeing "found" all those pocketbooks, I've been bag crazy. Gucci. Louis Vuitton. Fendi. Coach. You know I have them all, plus some other well-known names. Except Liz. Everybody has one of hers, so I didn't want any part of her initials. Anybody I'm dealing with knows which brand makes me weak at the knees.

"Oooh, Ange, that's phat. Try it on."

Grabbing a white crocheted two-piece and a lilac one, we went to the dressing room.

"Can you see anything?" Ange pranced around me. "Does it cover what it needs to?"

"Yeah. It looks good. Makes your boobs look bigger too."

"Then I'll take it!" Ange laughed.

Hardly a surfboard, Ange was a nice B. But she wanted Cs, or a D like me. She was even thinkin' about buying some. 'Cause you know in her world, everything can be bought and paid for. Years ago, Isabella had it done, so Ange thought Mr. Rinaldi wouldn't have any problems footing her bill.

We paid for the suits, then checked out the bags. A lime green backpack-style pocketbook was calling my name. It was made by Coach. Not a bad price, under two hundred dollars.

"If you like it, get it," Ange urged.

"I'm a little short today. Damon and I will have to have some pillow talk."

We browsed through some more stores and eventually got bored with shopping. Actually, we should have gone to one of the malls, Franklin Mills or even King of Prussia. They have more stores and I almost always find a fly bag that I can buy on the spot. With our shopping

49

done, we left—got back in the Honda and headed to the courts. Truly they would be jumpin'. Even though I was still mad at Damon, I was hoping I'd see him there. I had some words I wanted to throw in his face. Actin' like his cell phone died. I'm not stupid! And I wanted him to know I wasn't too. I just couldn't think of the best way to step to him about it. Damon only takes but so much heat. Coming at him was like treading water. I had to be careful, watch my words, pace myself so as not to get in too deep. He could be moody, and oftentimes the way he snapped at me hurt my feelings. I never told him that, though. But sometimes he talked to me like he didn't even care. I wasn't in the mood for having to protect my ego. I wanted to say my piece, let him know I know what's up, *and* I wanted that Coach bag. Only, Damon and his boyees weren't at the courts.

However, somebody else was! Austin Stewart III. His shirt was off and he was showing a nicely toned chest. Mmm, running up and down the basketball court hoopin'. The sun was dancing on Austin's muscular body. He looked hot in every sense of the word.

Settling on a bench by the court, I said, "Ange, let's watch this game."

"All right, but you know you don't care about basketball. You're just checking out Austin."

"Shut up, Ange." I laughed as I casually looked

around to make sure no one heard her. Ange can be loud!

Austin's team lost. Another team had next. Sweaty and smelly, Austin walked off the blacktop and toward us.

Cracking my gum, I said, "Hey, Austin," while glancing at his arms.

Using the shirt in his hand, he wiped the sweat. "What's up, Sheree? Angela?" Austin said.

I watched as more beads formed on his chest.

"Hi, Austin," Ange happily greeted him.

"You finished playin' for good? Whatchu doin' tonight?" I asked.

"We're gonna run again." Wiping more sweat. "So what's up with you, Angela? What have you been doing all summer?"

Quickly, I answered, "Me and Ange are just chillin'." Looking into his eyes, I asked again, "So what are you doin' later?"

He moved closer to Ange and said, "Angela? Does Sheree always speak for you?"

Ange laughed. "No, you know Sheree."

Then Austin laughed.

Defensively, I asked Austin, "What are you laughin' at?" Then I moved closer to him. His good looks were masking the stench and sweat rolling off of his body. Looking into his brown eyes, I said, "No, Ange, Austin doesn't know me. I keep givin' him chances and he

51

keeps runnin' away. I think he's scared." Invading his space, I urged him to accept my invitation. "Are you scared of *this*, Austin?"

"Yeah! Petrified!" He stood his ground, smiled, and said, "Why would I want something you're always throwin' away?"

See what I mean? Austin can be ignorant sometimes. He makes it hard for me to even like him a little bit. Seething, I sat back down on the bench. Despite my rolling eyes, Austin stood there talking; it was mostly to Ange, though. I was no longer interested in his conversation. Or his time.

"C'mon, Ange," I huffed. "Let's get going."

Ange willingly walked away. But then a few other guys stopped to talk to us. They weren't foolin' nobody. They were tryin' to push up on Ange. Several faces looked disappointed once they learned she had a man. As if on cue, Raheem rang her cellie.

"Hey, Raheem! I was just talking about you . . . to some people from my school. At the basketball courts with Sheree. Nothing, really. . . . Why? . . . What's up? . . . Um . . . uh-huh. . . . Well, I got, like, half that right now. . . . When do you need it? . . . I'll bring it tonight, then. . . . Oh, well . . . um hum . . . I can't come down tomorrow. . . . It's Sunday, you know we go to my nana's for dinner. . . . Just meet me tonight for a few minutes. . . . Well, I can meet you there. . . . Oh, all right. . . . Monday, then. . . . I love you too. . . . Be good. . . . Miss me? . . . Tell Rah-sool I said hi. . . . Tell me you love me again. . . . Me too. . . . Bye, Raheem."

Once we were far enough away from the group of guys, Ange told me what Raheem wanted. No surprise. He needed to borrow some money. The what-fors and promises of payback went in one ear and out my other. It didn't matter. No matter what I told Ange, she would still do as she pleased, and that was to give Raheem the money.

Just as we were about to leave the playground, who should walk through the fence? Damon. Dressed in a long tan linen button-down, short-sleeve shirt, with matching extra long pants and brown sandals. My man looked good! Lookin' like that, how could I be mad at him? As usual, everyone was checkin' his gear. I was smiling from ear to ear, thinkin' he was trying to impress me.

"You're lookin' good, Boo," I said as I moved real close to Damon, reminding all the girls to back off, Damon was mine.

"You too, baby girl," he said as he kind of stepped back, away from me. My eyes caught him checking out my tennis skirt and halter top. "Hey, Angela," he said.

Ange smiled. "Hi, Damon."

Casually surveying the playground, Damon put some butter in his voice. "Look, um, Sheree." He looked around again. "Where you gonna be at later?"

The disappointment in my voice was hidden by the cool attitude I projected. With one hand on my hip and my lips turned up, I cracked my gum and answered, "I don't know. Why?"

I know why and it's the same thing all the time.

"'Cause I got some things to take care of right quick. I'm'a stop by around nine. Be home! Put on that pink thing you have. See you then."

A quick kiss on the cheek and Damon walked away toward Bird. No asking me if he could come by the crib. As usual, I was expected to just listen and do. Fortunately, the kiss chilled some of the attitude. The disappointment was buried with the others. Like a fool, I thought he might want to hang out with me, go somewhere, and do something other than that. But no, he wanted to be with his boys!

"Whatchu want to do, Ange?"

"I got the munchies. Let's get something to eat."

Just the two of us went to Bella Italia for some pizza, but we saw lots of people from school there. After saying hello to some of our classmates, Ange and I settled into a booth. Between the two of us, our hurts, disappointments, and failures were safely allowed to resurface.

"I hate it when Raheem acts like he has to be with his friends and doesn't have time for me. I know he loves me, but he gets on my nerves with that. And then he's like, okay, lend me one hundred dollars, but don't bring it to me until Monday. He needs the money, right? So why doesn't he come up here to get it?"

"I know, Damon's the same way! Him and his boy-ees always have 'bidness to handle.' Only time he seems to have time for me is when he wants some."

"Why do we put up with them?"

"'Cause they're all the same." I took another slice of pizza.

"I love Raheem. Deep down, I think he'll change."

I stopped sprinkling the red pepper and looked at Ange seriously, wanting her to really understand my words. "Deep down, you know he's never gonna change," I suggested.

Staring right back at me, she threw it back. "You think Damon will change?"

I didn't even need to think. "Nope." I stared at the tiny white spots on the pepperoni on my plate. "No, I don't think Damon will change. But like you, I hope he will. I keep hoping that he'll see how I am the best thing he's got."

Ange pressed. "And if he doesn't?"

I looked back up at her. "He doesn't," I sighed.

For the next few minutes, we ate silently. Ange's voice brought me back to the restaurant.

"Well, Daddy noticed his Grand Marnier was missing."

"Aw, snap! What did he say to you?"

"Nothing."

"Nothing?"

"Not a thing! I heard him talking to Mom about it. He knows she hates that stuff so she didn't drink it. And that was it. See, I told you."

Yeah, Ange called it right. On the last day of school, Ange had a little party at her house. Isabella and Mr. Rinaldi were in Aruba for their wedding anniversary. Although Tony was home and was supposed to be keeping Ange company, he was into his own thing and never around. So with the house basically to herself, Ange had some friends over to drink and swim.

A few of the cool kids who knew how to party came. Moms, that means the house was full of mostly white folks, and me, Raheem, Russell, and Damon added the color. One thing I learned from hangin' with Ange is white people know how to P-arty too. But it's different from ours. Loud music, but no dancin'. They have beer, some hard liquor maybe, and lots of drugs.

People think only black people do drugs. I guess it's 'cause we're the only ones paraded on the TV news getting caught sellin'. And some of us use, too. But for real, these antidrug messages are twisted. From what I've seen with my own eyes, nobody black I know is doin' all that stuff. Ecstasy, angel dust, whippits—no way. Can't afford it! Ain't no rich daddies in the hood. We smokes weed—that's it, and it's cheap.

Good thing you gave me the drug talk long ago, because if I didn't watch out, I could get caught up at a party like Ange's. Like most Lower Harriton parties, there was a smorgasbord of drugs. Several people, especially those who didn't even look like they would partake, did. I bet some teachers and parents would be shocked to see who was licking this stamp, dropping that, or snorting this.

Anyway, Ange brought Raheem and Russell to her party. Yep, she had to pick them up and take them home the next day. I know, triflin'. They couldn't even take the train or bus. Oh, and for once Damon even came through, hooking us up with a couple of cases of beer and wine coolers. Damon even stayed at Ange's for a while with me. That was our first time really kickin' it, alone, without his boyees. Giving him a tour as if it were my own, I showed Damon Ange's house. He was impressed. Started talking big. Talking about how he's gonna buy a forty-two-inch plasma TV too. And also have his whole house wired for music and computers.

Yeah, Damon got quite comfortable in the Rinaldis' digs, sayin' how this was how he was gonna live in a few years. Someone offered him a beer, but he schooled us all on how a man like him gets down. No beer, no wine coolers. Just top shelf. So Ange went into the bar in the basement and got Mr. Rinaldi's Grand Marnier. I told her that wasn't a good idea. But she said, "Sheree, I could walk in the house with purple hair and Daddy wouldn't notice anything. And if he does, he definitely won't think I drank it."

So Damon, Raheem, and Russell became fast friends that night over a newly opened bottle of Grand Marnier. Talking loudly, joking, playin' Dominoes, they downed it all. Neither Ange nor I drank it because it tasted so nasty.

Using some of the money Damon gave me, I paid the bill at Bella Italia. Ange and I usually take turns treating. When I got money, it's Ange's. If she needs it, it's hers. I told you how deep Ange's pockets are, and she really is quite generous, but I refuse to take advantage of my friend. Raheem already does enough of that.

We had to make it an early night because Damon said he'd be by around nine. I wanted to be home by eight thirty just in case he was early. After dropping me off at home, Ange was also turning in early.

9:15 . . . 9:30 . . . 10:00 . . . 10:30 . . . 10:45 . . . 11:00. As the minutes passed, I grew angrier. I was beginning to think that I should never trust someone who doesn't wear a watch. How's he gonna have me sittin' waiting for him? At eleven fifteen someone knocked on the door. It was Damon. I shouldn't have answered it. It would've served him right! But I couldn't ignore him any more than I could ignore my own desires.

"You're late," I snapped gently.

"Late, but here. You're not happy to see me? I can leave."

Knowing he'd walk back out the door and into God knows where, I quickly dropped the attitude. And I showed him how much I missed him.

When we were done, I played the pretend game. Only I had to play it by myself. Damon doesn't like my version. I don't particularly care for his, either.

I pretend we're grown and married. We are deeply in love and have two kids. A boy named Damon Junior and a pretty little long-haired girl named Demeree. (It's a combination of both of our names.) We live in a big house like Ange's, and have a swimming pool and a four-car garage.

Once when I shared this with Damon, he said, "I don't want no more kids, Sheree."

He already had two boys. Two-year-old Tyler, and Damon Junior, or DJ, who is like five or six months old. Thank God, neither of their mamas lives in Ardmore. The only time Damon sees the boys is when their moms take them to visit Damon's mom, Ms. Joyce.

Okay, so no kids. But Damon never said no to getting married. He just laughed at that part.

I joined him in that laugh. Secretly. Because that was all I could do in *his* pretend game. He wanted to open a combination chicken and rib stand, barber shop, and hair salon. Ain't that funny, Moms? Why? 'Cause, Moms, Damon can't cook. He's never cooked chicken, ribs, bacon, or eggs. And he couldn't even barbecue, let alone make some slammin' sauce. Also, he couldn't cut hair! And what did he know about runnin' a business? Nothing. He knew the pharmaceutical business, I'll give him that. But that was it.

This was how I really knew it wouldn't work: Who wanted to get their hair "did" where they are going to come out smelling like barbecue sauce? Shoot, if it weren't for all that sheen sprayed on our hair, we'd smell like burned hair. Can't no woman stand that burnt smell. Some girls be trippin' off of the sweet smell of sheen. So imagine barbecue sauce? No, no, that ain't gonna work.

You know why I really didn't play pretend with Damon no more, though? Sometimes I wondered if *I* was his game. Was he pretending with me, too? He never said he loved me. I guess I didn't really expect him to say that anyway. That was not exactly his style. But sometimes I felt like deep down he probably did. He was there, right? He came over. He gave me money. He was nice to me, you, and my friends. Is that love?

But sometimes, I just didn't know what to think. Damon would see me walkin' and sometimes he would just toot his horn and drive by. He wouldn't even stop to say hi or give me a lift or nothin'. What's up with that? He wouldn't want me coming over his house. Supposedly Ms. Joyce was funny that way. She wouldn't want a lot of people in her house, so he couldn't have company. But Damon was a grown man; that didn't make sense. Besides, Ms. Joyce let those other girls bring their little rug rats over for a visit. And then there was this: I always had to call him on his cell phone, not the number at his mom's house. I didn't even know it; it was unlisted.

After sitting around for a few, I could tell Damon was getting restless. He was looking for a quick exit without starting an argument. His cell phone saved him.

"Talk to me," he said to the caller. "In a few. Be cool. I'm on my way. I'm just finishing up some bidness."

Oh, so I'm bidness now, I thought as I watched him thinking he could mack on his cell right in front of me.

"Soon. Holla," he said, shutting the cell phone.

This time an argument was unavoidable!

"Who was that?" I asked.

Damon was mute.

Watching my tone and my neck, "Who was that?" I carefully demanded.

"Girl, calm down. That was just Bird." Damon tried to laugh and massage my shoulders.

I moved away and surprised myself by shouting, "Damon? Do I look like Boo Boo the Clown? You don't talk to Bird, Chris, or none of your boys like that! So who's this chick?"

"Look, Sheree, I told you it was Bird. I'm not in the mood for this drama. Now don't come at me like that. You hear? Save *that* for those young bucks. It was Bird and that's it."

From experience, I knew that in his mind this conversation was over. Quickly, I weighed my options. Continue to fight? No, he'd never tell me who really on the phone anyway. He told the caller he was finishing up some bidness. Normally Damon would have told his boys he was with me, so I decided to handle him as a "bidness" transaction.

Making adjustments, I pushed attitude to hang out with disappointment. "Um, Damon?" I settled my body right in his face. "I'm a little short. I saw this bad Coach bag at the mall. I know you'll love it."

Easy. Realizing he was off the hook, Damon reached into his wallet. Then he left.

This time I was happy to see him do so. He wasn't making a fool out of me. I was on to him. And her? I wondered if it was Miss Marci who lived on Simpson Road. Lately she seemed to be all up in his chocolate face. I thought she was just buying, but maybe they'd got something goin' on. Miss Marci was way older than Damon. She was, like, thirty or something. But like you, Moms, she kept herself up. But, nah, it couldn't have been Miss Marci. She may have been tryin' to throw it at Damon and he may have dipped in there, but she was not his type. She was too old! Shoot, Damon didn't even holla at chicks his own age. He liked them like me. Late teens with a mature body and grown attitude. So if it wasn't Miss Marci, who could it be?

Although I wanted to know the name of this mystery chick, I wasn't gonna lose any sleep over her. You taught me that, right? Tears are wasted energy.

Yeah, you taught me that one back in middle school. I was in the sixth grade and had been goin' with Timmy, who was in the eighth. He was my first. After he got it a couple of times, he quit me. My first one, my first heartbreak. Timmy didn't even tell me to my face. Calling out of the blue, since we weren't girls no more, Jemina dropped the dime.

"Hey, Sheree," Jemina said.

"Jemina? Hey, what you want?" I figured she must have needed something to be calling me. Although we still spoke and exchanged some words from time to time, that was it. We weren't like we used to be. I was hoping this call, whatever the purpose, was her makin' up with me.

"Sheree, you and Timmy are still together, right?"

Uh-oh, a feeling of dread overcame me. I began twirling the phone cord in your room. Taking a deep breath, I answered, "Yeah. Why?"

Anticipating the worst, knowing . . . waiting for the news.

"'Cause, he asked Raquel to the eighth-grade dinner dance. And she says they're also messin' with each other and that he broke up with you."

"He didn't quit me!" Relief. "Raquel is lyin'." Thinkin' that perhaps this was all a big misunderstanding, some of the feelings of doom left me. Raquel was probably just jealous. She liked Timmy. She was tryin' to cause problems.

Jemina explained. "No, Sheree, Raquel's not playin' Pinocchio. I asked Timmy myself. He said he's not with you no more; he's moved on to Raquel."

All of the anxious feelings returned. This couldn't be true. Jemina was lyin' too. She was just jealous because of what happened between me and her the year before. This was her payback. I told her I had to go, hung up the phone, and called Timmy.

"Uh, Timmy, I'm hearin' some things about you and Raquel," I said.

"Yeah, and?" he answered.

"Well, aren't you takin' me to the eighth-grade dinner dance? Me and Moms are supposed to get a dress next week when she gets paid."

"Well . . . uh . . . uh . . . you see, um . . . my mom . . ."

Hurt and annoyed, I yelled, "What, Timmy? Spit it out!"

Backed into a corner, he fired back, "No. I'm takin' Raquel and I go with her now too."

The dreadful feelings were replaced by sadness. I tried to hold back. Didn't want him to hear me cry. Struggling to keep the tears locked, my loud voice squeaked, "What? So that's it? It's over between us?"

Calmly he answered, "Yeah, and um . . . don't call

here anymore. . . . Um . . . my mom . . ."

He was still running his jowls as I slammed the phone down. I couldn't believe it! Like that, we were through and now he was going to be with Raquel. Jemina wasn't lyin'. I bet she just loved calling me up breaking the news and now spreading it. As the realization of me and Timmy being over hit, I threw myself onto your bed, burying my face in your pillow, crying and screaming. Why? Why? Why?

A question you wanted answered too. Why was I crying? What was wrong with me? What happened? Hopelessly feeling like all of my friends were now laughin' at me after they warned me not to give it up to Timmy, I told you what was wrong. I thought that maybe you could help make everything right again. Not able to undo what was done, you quickly schooled me.

"Oh, Ree Ree." Your laughter confused me. It seemed to be mixed with annoyance and yet understanding. "Ree Ree, I don't want to see you crying over no boys! Since the beginning of time, that's what boys have done. They chase you, talk that sweet stuff, get some, get bored, and move on. If you're smart, you don't give them your heart, 'cause they never give theirs. *Never* care more for them than they do for you. Always keep something for yourself. And that something has to be your heart. If you do that, you'll never want to cry again. But maybe, just maybe, if you handle them right, they'll cry for you."

That was the first and last time I cried over a guy. Since then, my heart has been carefully protected— guarded like a Brink's truck, silently wishing the lure of what was inside would attract a robber. As I get older, I realize no one would really even have to steal it. I am ready to give. But a locksmith or a robber hasn't shown his face. Passing time, waiting, doing it your way . . . juicin' 'em.

So, with your lessons learned, I didn't fret about Damon's mystery chick. As long as I continued to get some of what I wanted, it was all good. I went upstairs, locked my door, and went to sleep. I didn't hear you come home.

The next morning your door was open and your bed untouched. It was obvious that you didn't come home. I wondered where you were. But I have awakened to your absence enough times to know not to be concerned. Eventually, you would present yourself.

Time flew by and still no you. At about three o'clock, I started to worry. The first person I called was Candy. She forgot to call me! You asked her to be the bearer of news. I'm sure if I had just walked outside I would have learned too. Someone would have had something to say. Someone would have been talkin' smack about how they seen it all at Regal's. But Candy was the one to tell me that you were in jail.

You and Miss Phyllis. Miss Phyllis? Locked up for fighting. Candy said it started because Miss Phyllis's man, Smoky, kept talkin' to you, buying you drinks. Miss Phyllis started it, but you finished it, getting the best of her. Police were called and both of y'all were taken away in handcuffs.

I grabbed some money and ran to the police station. It was Sunday. Gorgeous outside. The man at the desk looked like he wanted to be anywhere but at work. And since he was at work, he seemed to be determined to make everyone feel as miserable as he did. He wasn't helpful. No matter what lies I said . . . sick . . . hasn't seen me . . . from out of town . . . he wouldn't let me see you. After a while, he gave me a slip of paper with the district justice's address and the time you would appear in court the next day. Frustrated, I walked back home.

I knew you would be okay. It was just one more night. It was only jail and not prison. But I also knew you hated being enclosed. I wondered if you and Miss Phyllis were in the same cell.

I also wondered why you would even be bothered

with Smoky. Everybody knew he was crazy! He was always beatin' up Miss Phyllis. I heard they had some WWE-type smack downs, with Miss Phyllis putting in some licks too. She was just as crazy as Smoky. And, c'mon, Moms, Smoky wasn't even your type. You wouldn't let anybody play OJ on you or your body.

At home I began searching the house for more money. I had no idea what your bail would be. I just knew that I wouldn't be able to buy the bag I wanted. For a moment I thought of calling Mom Mom.

She'd have some money; only, you wouldn't want to repay that debt. This would just be another thing Mom Mom would hold over your head. So I didn't call her. And I definitely didn't ring Roc. Even though he was my dad, you wouldn't want him in your bidness either. Candy? Maybe she could have loaned us a couple of dollars. But it would have been small change. She still owed you some money from the last week. No, that left me with two choices: Ange and Damon.

Actually, I really only had one choice. I didn't want to ask Ange for any money. If I absolutely had to, then I would, but it would be my last resort.

Damon was the only person left. I hit him on his cell.

"Hey, Boo. Can we talk right quick? Did you hear about what happened at Regal's? . . . Yeah, she's still in there. I need some money for bail, maybe. I won't know until tomorrow how much it's gonna be. You got me or what? A'ight, den. You gonna bring it by later tonight? Cool. I'll be here. Okay. Bye, Boo."

As long as your bail wasn't over five hundred, you were coming home the next day.

Later that night, Damon dropped by and gave me three hundred-dollar bills. He was dressed to kill! Wearing a white linen suit without a shirt, I knew he was going somewhere. But I didn't even sweat him. In my mind I knew that whoever this chick was, she wasn't all that if Damon was still giving me the Benjamins.

If I'd never learned anything else, one of your early lessons I immediately understood. Nothing is for free. Like everything else in life, Damon's gift came with a price. I paid on my knees.

First thing Monday morning, I called Bryn Mawr Terrace Convalescent Center, telling your supervisor you were sick. I didn't want you to lose a day's pay, or worse, let you hear Trump's famous two words. Then I walked to the district justice's office. Yesterday at the police station, the man told me ten o'clock. I was at the DJ's by nine thirty, but no you. All morning I sat in that tiny lobby waiting for your case to be heard. Finally, Jemison. As the cop led you into the room, I stared at your tired eyes and messed-up do. Jail didn't look good on you.

The charges were read. Simple assault and disorderly conduct. Thankfully, the judge let me keep my money as you were allowed to leave on an ROR—released on your own recognizance. Silently, I cheered, *Hello, Coach!* You had a flash of hope in your eyes too. However, it was quickly dashed when you learned your fine. Six hundred dollars! Plus court costs! I thought, *Good-bye, lime green purse!*

After you agreed to the terms and signed the papers, you were set free. Free to go. Free to touch me. But somehow, we got it backward. The hug I embraced you with should have been the one you gave me. Once again, I found myself holdin' you down.

As much as I wanted to light into you for getting caught up like that, I couldn't. It seems you can tell me anything. Tell me about your boyfriends, how much they make, if they perform well, tell me neighborhood gossip, what happens at Regal's. Talk to me like I'm your sister or girlfriend. I am expected to listen with adult ears, but also supposed to remember my child's place and be quiet and not question. Not question you. So I held my tongue and listened as you ranted and raved.

No, it wasn't your fault. Smoky was tryin' to talk to you. Buy you a drink. Yeah, it was a free drink, why should you say no? You weren't even feelin' him with his long-headed self. Miss Phyllis didn't have to get all loud. She threw a drink in your face. Yeah, you had to teach the hussy a lesson. She was lucky your blade was at home. She better watch her back.

That last comment was when I had to jump in. "Moms, leave Miss Phyllis be. You don't want to get locked up again. And you definitely don't want no more fines."

For once, you actually considered my point. You agreed to let it die. As long as she stayed out of your face, you could forget.

When we got home, you rushed to erase the smell. A bath. Something to eat. I got on the phone to call Ange. I needed to get out of the house. While you were locked up, I was the one *cooped* up, worrying about you.

A little later, Ange picked me up. She needed to give Raheem his money. I didn't want to leave what *was* your bail money at home because I knew you'd take it and spend it, so I brought it with me. I wasn't going to buy the pocketbook, yet I planned to hold on to the money. I just didn't trust you with it, or knowing that I had it. From experience, I have learned that you enjoy spending mine and saving yours.

"Sheree, we have to make a stop first," Ange said as I shut the car door.

"Okay. Where?"

"Drugstore . . . I'm late."

My eyes got all big. Raising my voice above the music, I asked, "Ange? How late?"

"Three weeks."

Relieved, I said, "Oh, that ain't nothin'. I skipped twice. Maybe you just skipped too."

With certainty in her voice, Ange answered, "I never skip! I always come on the second week of the month, on a Wednesday at that."

Not so certain, I asked, "Well, whatchu think? How you feel?"

"I think I need to take a test."

We bought the test, the type with two kits in case we made a mistake. Since there weren't any public bathrooms in the drugstore, Ange had to do it at Raheem's house. No mistaking, one test was enough. The blue line showed in a matter of seconds.

Although Raheem tried to act unfazed, he looked a little nervous when Ange came out of the bathroom. However, when he heard the news, he acted like a proud papa-to-be.

"My baby's gonna have a baby!" He picked up Ange and swung her around.

Pulling away, Ange said, "I can't have a baby! Daddy will kill me! Then he'll kill you—limb from limb."

That dose of reality burst Raheem's bubble.

Putting her back on the ground, he asked, "So how are you gonna do this? I may be able to get, like, a hundred together."

I asked myself if that would be before or after he paid her back for the loan.

"I don't know." Then Ange started crying. A serious crybaby, she'd surprised me by keeping it together that long. Raheem pulled her close and stroked her hair.

Due to Raheem's constant money problems, I sometimes questioned his feelings for Ange. But as I watched him hug her, there was no doubting his feelings. They seemed to be legit. The question now was what to do about Ange's situation.

We hung out at Raheem's for a while, mostly sitting, listening to music, and watching the little girls outside jumping double Dutch. Two little nappy-headed boys kept messing with the group of girls. The competition begins! One girl reminded me of me. Since she was playing with girls who looked to be about ten, I thought she was probably the same age too. Only her body, just like mine did, was growing ahead of schedule. She already had big titties, a thick butt, and thunder thighs.

As the boys kept trying to grab her butt, I noticed the other girls' reaction. Instead of getting mad at the boys and chasing them away, they turned on the girl. It wasn't in an overly obvious way. But as someone who's been there before, it was easy enough for me to recognize.

Too bad the little girl didn't have long, thick plaits. Like me, her hair wasn't past her ears. When I was her age, I always wished for long hair. I was sure it would have taken the attention away from my body.

As I watched the girls play, I was certain the little girl knew the whispers and eye rollin' were directed at her. Where do little girls learn to be so mean? She pretended not to hear and see them. That's exactly how I lost my best friend, Jemina. When it was just me and her, Jemina was cool. But as soon as any boys came around, she would change up, treating me differently. All of a sudden, my name was "big tittie," "mountain girl," or "mounds of Sheree." And if we were jumping, rules quickly changed.

"No, don't let Sheree jump. It's not her turn," Jemina would say, all bossy. Knowing it was my turn, she'd order Tammy to jump next. Or, as soon as it was my turn, she'd end the game, say "they" (translation: Tammy, Dorinda, and Jemina) were going to do something else. I always ended up standing there, stuck with the boys.

If it had just been me and one of my so-called friends, it would have been a fair one. But knockin' bows with the three of them was out of the question. So I had to absorb it all. Who could I run to? You and Mom Mom would tell me to work it out myself. How?

I didn't ask those boys to touch my booty. Or flick my bra strap. Or grab my titties like they were headlights. I couldn't help that they called Jemina flat-chested. Tammy, ugly. Ignored Dorinda. Me and Jemina were best friends. I'd have done anything for her; she was my girl. But boys ruined it. Come to think of it, aren't boys always the cause of any two girlfriends fallin' out?

I desperately wished that I could spare this little girl's feelings. It hurts so bad when your best friend stops speaking to you. And that's the only way this little girl's situation is gonna play out.

It was fifth grade. The summer. Jemina and I were best friends, in the little-girl sense. One evening we were all at the playground sitting on the swings. It was me, Jemina, Tammy, and Dorinda. We were talkin' about Usher's new video, "My Way," when Marky and Bosco walked over. As the boys put their two cents into our conversation, I fell silent. Understanding the rules of friendship, I knew it was best not to say or do anything that might cause me to be singled out. My body brought enough unasked-for attention. So I kept my mouth shut, silently swinging, hoping they'd leave.

Boys always brought trouble. Always caused them—my friends—to turn on me. But there would be no such luck. Speakin' for all of us, Jemina agreed to play tag.

Tag? In fifth grade? Boys catch the girls? It sounded like a bad idea, but Dorinda and them were with it so I was down. Marky and Bosco were it. All of us girls took off in the same direction toward the trees by the tennis courts. Marky and Bosco were bookin'. Not wanting to be caught, I ran my fastest. Turning back, I could see Jemina barely running. She liked Marky and probably wanted him to catch her. He and Bosco ran right past. Past Dorinda and Tammy, too. They were gaining on me. Unable to fake out, like boys do, I could only run straight. Straight until I stumbled over a tree root and they caught me.

Palming my butt, Marky squeezed. This wasn't boys catch the girls. It was catch-a-girl-git-a-girl.

"Stop, Marky," I said, and swung to smack him.

Laughing, he dodged out of the way. Ever the copycat, Bosco tried doing the same. I was able to kick him in the shins.

"Aw, girl, stop it," Marky said as he kissed me while Bosco tried humping my butt.

Swinging my arms wildly, I got them to let me loose.

"Aw, go 'head, girl," Marky said as he and Bosco walked back toward the swings.

Huddled together, Jemina, Tammy, and Dorinda were whispering. I knew they were talking about me. Just as I knew who was doing the most talking, the ringleader, my girl Jemina. Cautiously, I approached their little circle. Clearly, they understood that I didn't ask for this. Marky and Bosco caught me. I fought back. I didn't like them. Jemina liked Marky. Dorinda, Bosco.

"I ain't playin' no more. They're nasty," I said, hoping to break the wall of silence that surrounded me.

Talking around me, Jemina told the others, "C'mon, let's go to my house. We [she looked right at me] don't play games like that."

Jemina stepped and the other two followed. I got the message; I wasn't welcome to come too. Standing there, alone, I wanted to run up to Jemina, Dorinda, and Tammy and call them out. Pull Tammy's long ponytail. Scratch up Jemina's pretty face. Punch Dorinda in her fat stomach. But I didn't. I figured it would all blow over; we'd all be cool again, tomorrow.

Tomorrow, and the day after that and the days after those, we were never girls again. They stopped talkin' to me. Even Jemina. It was lonely. Talk about summers dragging on. Without anyone to play with, summer seemed to last years. And as I watched this little girl playin' double Dutch, I wanted to warn her—warn her of what was coming, tell her my story. In a few years the jealous girls would stop whispering and just start boldly talking, calling her a ho, skeezer, or slut. She has to let those names roll off of her back. Step on 'em. Maybe I should warn this little girl's friends, too—warn them of what's coming their way. Tell them how this little girl has the power to flip the script. Just like I did. . . .

In eighth grade Jemina and I were acquaintances. Friend? Girl? Homey? Not words reserved for her no more. Although we weren't close, I still heard mumblings about what she was up to, who she liked: Bilal. Bilal King was a ninth grader and at the high school already. Jemina liked him and liked him bad. Every day she'd wait after school for the activity bus, tryin' to sit with him. Dressin' in her flyest gear, she hoped to catch his eye.

Personally, I didn't see what she saw in him. He was okay. I mean real okay-lookin'. Nothin' at all special. He was my height, so that was too short for me. Plus, somethin' about him was sketchy. But hey, Jemina liked him, so I *wanted* him. And I put it on him. Snatching him and sportin' him in front of her. Pulling Bilal was easy. Too easy. Never having had a girlfriend before, he was ready to come.

Jemina was too through. But what could she do? Bilal was mine. All those times she, Tammy, and them used to tease me, give me the silent treatment, all of that was worth taking Bilal from her. Although he didn't look like much, Bilal became my grand prize.

But I kept my stories to myself. Kept my butt seated on Raheem's aluminum folding chair. No cautionary tales were told by me. No, this little girl jumping double Dutch would just have to deal. Like I had to.

Meantime, Ange's problem still wasn't solved. But Raheem needed us to be out before his mom got home at midnight. She was on a different shift. Driving back to Ardmore, Ange and I talked some more. She had a serious dilemma. She didn't want to have a baby, but she was scared to get an abortion.

Turning down the radio, I said, "Ange, I had an abortion before."

"You did? When?" Ange pulled the car over to the side of the road.

I went on to tell her about my first, Timmy. If I knew then what I know now, he would have never been my first. But I was twelve years old. Young and stupid! I actually believed that you couldn't get pregnant your first time doin' it. Duh! Yeah, I know, Moms, you told me otherwise! But I was young, so I believed him. Well, I did it. Did it a couple of times, too. And yes, I got pregnant.

I told Ange how you quirked out, calling me some of the same names my old girlfriends did. It stung more when you said it, though. But you solved my problem.

Taking me to the clinic. Two days later, walking through the right-to-lifers, who chanted "baby killer" (how did they know what I was there for?), we entered the clinic and got it done.

"Did it hurt? Were you put to sleep?" Ange asked.

"I was awake the whole time. The doctor gave me some shot that numbed everything down there. I didn't feel pain as much as I felt pressure. It felt like someone was tugging on me."

Ange looked away. "Oh." Sliding down her cheek, one lone tear. Turning the radio back up, Ange guided the car back onto the road.

What I didn't tell Ange was what I felt afterward. Nothing! I felt nothing. What happens afterward is always brushed under the rug. Oh, I was a little sore from the procedure. And I bled a lot. I was expecting that; the nurse at the clinic prepared me for it. But the emotions? Or lack of them? No one told me I might not feel anything inside. Empty. It was surreal. Like all of that didn't really happen to me. Like okay, that's done, now can I go back to being a twelve-year-old?

Today, the fact that I felt nothing haunts my thoughts. I wondered how I was able to kill a part of me. I often wonder if it was a girl. Or a boy. Or both maybe. Whatever it was, it would have been five years old now.

As we pulled up in front of the house, I clicked the radio off, shutting down Power's most-requested list. I didn't need to know the station's number one. I needed to talk to my girl. So I asked, "Ange, what are you gonna do?"

Sadly, she answered, "I don't know. I just don't know." A couple more tears freely raced down her cheek.

"All right. Well, I'm here for you." I hugged her. "You know whatever I got, it's yours if you need it. Call me tomorrow. Bye."

The summer days dragged on. As the temperature continued to climb, your attitude got funkier. It started with your court notice. You had to appear before the judge and either plead guilty or go to trial. Opting to skip the Judge Judy route and just pay the six-hundred-dollar fine and court costs, you planned to plead guilty. Your decision. Your fine. So why did I have to help pay the price again? I didn't get arrested.

One afternoon in the kitchen, you stated your position. "Sheree, you're gonna have to get a job or something to help pay this six-hundred-dollar bill."

Resisting the urge to roll my eyes, I said, "Moms, it's a fine, not a bill."

"Fine. Bill. Same thing! It's six hundred we don't

got. You're off all summer. Ain't got a job. Complaining 'cause there ain't food in the house, but you don't buy nothin' your damn self. You need to get off your butt and get a job! They're hiring right now at Bryn Mawr Terrace Convalescent Center. Here," you said while pulling something out of your purse. "Here's an application."

Out of respect or fear, I grabbed the piece of paper and mumbled, "Fine." However, I was feeling anything but that. I needed to escape. Get away. Storming out of the house, I hoped the streets would cool me.

You know, Moms, even though I didn't have a job, I always gave you some money. Sometimes, half of what I had! No matter how much I gave, it never seemed to be enough, though. I'd get a job. I knew how to work. I wasn't lazy. Shoot, you've collected unemployment and disability before. So, I'd find a job. *BUT!* But not at Bryn Mawr Terrace. There was no way I was cleaning up after old people. I'd work at the mall, or even KFC if I had to.

I tried to stay out as long as I could that day. Away from you. But as night fell, there was no escape from the humidity. So I dragged my butt home hoping that was enough time for you to cool down.

Sitting on the couch, smoking a cigarette, watching TV, you greeted me, "Roc came by."

His name brightened up my mood. Just like that, I was smiling and happy, forgetting about our argument. Excitedly, I asked, "He did? What for?"

The look on your face told me that my happiness was hurting you. It's a look I've seen before, every time you mentioned Roc. Despite that, you answered my question. "He said he was over this way, and he stopped in to see you."

I slumped in the chair. "Dag, I was only right around the corner too. Why didn't he come by the courts? How long did he stay?"

"Not long." Blowing cigarette smoke out of your mouth, you said, "I put his ass out!"

I thought, *Here we go again!*

Like a little girl, I whined, "Why, Moms?"

Smashing the cigarette into the ashtray, you gave your side. "He heard about what happened at Regal's and he started talkin' that stuff, like he's runnin' thangs. I told him he don't pay any bills up in here. So he ain't got shit to say about how I act. Then I said you wasn't here, so good-bye."

Couldn't you have kept your mouth shut? Just for me? It seems like you always come between Roc and me. I don't get it. He's my dad. I know y'all still got beef, but can't you squash it for me? He only lives one town over, but our visits, if you can call them that, are far and wide.

The disappointment must have been showing on my face. I know my lips were pokin' out. As I was taught to do, I swallowed what I was feelin' inside. I take it you saw it all, because you lost your angry tone.

"Oh, Ree Ree, I told him to come by tomorrow morning after I leave for work." A mixture of sadness and disgust was in your voice.

A smile quickly replaced my frown. Feeling generous, I said, "Here, Moms. Here's four hundred for your fine." I hugged you tightly.

As usual, you didn't ask me any questions. You grabbed the money, hugging me back. I guess you knew Damon gave it to me. There was no more talk about getting a job.

The next morning, I was showered and dressed before six. That was early for me. I wanted to look good for Roc. At first I waited on the stoop, watering the flowers, then deadheading the mini rosebush kept me busy for a while. Eventually, I got bored and went back inside. I watched . . . *Dr. Phil*, *All My Children*, *One Life to Live*, *General Hospital*, and *TRL*. Still, no Roc!

It was the same thing happening to me again—Roc making empty promises. The year before, after having some type of Oprah aha moment, Roc said he would try to spend more time with me. He said he was tryin' to be a better dad. Now look at him. Is this what fathers do?

Talk, talk, talk. Wasn't that all you said he ever did?

I wasted the day waiting for him. A part of me wanted to call him up and curse him out, but I feared doing that would keep him away. Then I got angry with you. I wondered if you really told him to come back, or if you had me sittin' around like a fool? No, you can sometimes do some wacked things, but I know you would never do that.

No, this was all Roc. He always pulled this, says he's gonna come by, or take me out, and then never shows. Why did I keep fallin' for this? Why was I dressed up for a man who never kept his promises?

As much as I wanted to leave the house, perhaps find Damon or hang out with Ange, I couldn't go farther than the front stoop. My body was paralyzed. It clung to the hope—desire? chance?—that Roc might appear, or even call.

In the early evening, when you came home from work, I was fixed in the same position, sitting back on the stoop. I hadn't had a cigarette all day, so I was dying. Roc hates cigarettes, especially the lingering smell, so I always wonder if that's why you and he split. If I knew I was gonna see Roc, I made sure he couldn't smell any tobacco or even weed on me.

As you walked up the steps, I was embarrassed

when you saw me still sitting there. Waiting. Played again. This time there was no need for you to question me. My eyes answered your unasked question. Thankfully, you didn't run Roc down into the ground. You walked inside and changed out of your uniform. I remained on the stoop for a while.

Later, I came in, made myself something to eat, and sat in the front room. My body wouldn't move far from the telephone or the door. Just in case he stopped by, I wanted to be able to answer it. Open the door before he walked away. And if he called? I could be the first one to grab the phone, before you, or before he hung up.

In my heart, I knew. I knew when Erica Kane came on the screen. I knew he wasn't really coming. Roc has to be at work at twelve. So why did I continue to sit? Despite what I knew, something inside me wouldn't let me go on. For one day, everything in my world stopped. Stopped. Hoped. And waited.

As the Cinderella hour approached, Roc's grasp loosened. I was finally able to move more than five feet, walking upstairs to go to bed. Before resting my head, I did what I was dying to do all day: have a cigarette. The first puff was the best. Like a Hoover vacuum cleaner, I sucked, holding it as long as I could.

Holding it was holding me together. Eventually reality hit. I needed air just as much as I needed to cry. Breathing came easier; it was more natural.

I slept with a lump in my throat.

Several weeks dragged by before I saw Ange again. It took her a few days and lots of courage to tell Isabella. Although Isabella was disappointed, she kept Ange's situation under wraps from Mr. Rinaldi.

Mother and daughter went to the doctor to take another pregnancy test. I guess the one from the drugstore wasn't considered reliable enough for the doctor. Yeah, she was pregnant. About two months.

Two days later, they left early in the morning— Isabella and Ange—hours before Mr. Rinaldi went to work. Without raising suspicion, they told him they had hair appointments. At six in the morning? He never questioned. I heard he never even raised one of his thick eyebrows. He was probably just happy that they would be out of his sight. When Mr. Rinaldi came home from work that night, he also didn't question either of them about their uncut hair looking the same. Or that his "princess" seemed to be so tired and irritable.

Ever fearful of pain, Ange was put to sleep. She was in at seven thirty and released by ten. The aftereffects of the anesthesia caused Ange to throw up all over the kitchen floor. Eleanor cleaned up the mess while Isabella tended to Ange.

Although Ange said she felt fine, Isabella hadn't really left her side. For three weeks she babied Ange, not letting her leave the house, drive, stick her toes into their pool—barely allowing her to talk on the phone. After some serious begging on Ange's part, I was eventually allowed to visit. We shut ourselves in her bedroom, away from Isabella.

"Have you heard from Raheem yet?" I asked.

"Yeah. When Mom went to the store, I called him. He was worried about me. He wanted to know how I felt. He said how much he loved me. And then he said how he was scared to call me. I cried and told him that was stupid. He wants to get a place of his own, so when I graduate, we can live together."

Not believing Raheem's fairy tale, I stuck to the real world. "Did he get a job yet? How's he gonna pay rent?"

"He's thinking about going back to school. He says he just has to do about a year or so and then he'll get his degree. Sheree, he sounded so sad on the phone. I can't wait until Mom will let me leave this house! The doctor told me to take it easy for a few days. It's been three weeks; this is ridiculous. She is driving me crazy!"

"Yeah, well, you know Isabella."

I'd known Isabella for less than a year. In that short time, I figured some things out about her. She didn't seem to pay Ange or Tony much attention. Oh, she made sure they were clothed and fed. Their physical needs were met and met well. But that was all. It seemed to be all Isabella was able to give. That is, until either one of them got sick.

Sickness brought out the mother in Isabella. Too much mother. Put an *s* in front of that word and that's what she did to Ange and Tony, but only when they weren't feeling well, forcing them to choose defensive positions: fight or flight? Tony ran, often hiding his bumps, bruises, and illnesses. Today, Ange was battling. Choking the anger, which secretly burned in her heart, she no longer wanted to be coddled by Isabella. She didn't want her mother on those terms any longer. This war actually began our junior year when Ange stopped being so sick. All through middle school and darn near most of high school, some unknown ailment always seemed to plague her, keeping her out of school for days on end. She wasn't a hypochondriac either! There's probably a medical name for someone who craves her mother's love. It's just that her doctors could never find the source of her so-called pains.

And Mr. Rinaldi? Well, he's more consistent with his lack of attention. Medical emergencies, good report cards, and ballet recitals barely raised an eyebrow. He basically told Ange and Isabella, no more. No more doctors. No more specialists. At the beginning of our junior year, he ordered Ange to stay in school. No more sick days. And so she did.

Isabella? Silently, she slipped back into her own world. A world filled with personal training sessions at the gym. Manicures. Pedicures. Hair appointments. Shopping sprees. Occasional drug use. Isabella prefers white lines. Lunches with girlfriends. Like me, Ange is often upgraded to that role. Isabella uses her as a sounding board—complaining about Mr. Rinaldi, the long hours he spends at work, his affair with some lady at their country club, why she can't leave him.

Smoke and mirrors. Until I got to know Isabella, I thought she had it made. The perfect life. A big house. Not one, but two walk-in closets full of nice clothes. More than thirty purses. Obviously, her gear was expensive too. She was like a sista, changing her hair color as often as she changed her nail polish. She had a rich husband who owned his own business. A maid. Who could ask for more? However, none of that seemed to really make her happy. She smiled all the time, but it was forced and fake, like underneath her bought tan, she was really crying. She was too skinny, too. I never saw her grubbing on the pasta dishes, whose smells often permeated the house. So maybe what everyone says is true: Money doesn't buy happiness. Although I'd love to test that theory! Maybe that was what Isabella discovered. Perhaps dealing with that realization was what kept her in her own world—a world where her children may visit with their ailments, but once healed, must leave.

So where does that leave Ange? It used to leave her on the outside, devising ways to get in, inventing stomach aches, migraines, and breathing problems. But now Ange allows Isabella to return to her insulated space. Ange found her own universe. She found Raheem.

"So, Ange, are you gonna finally go on the pill?"

"Uh-uh." She shook her head. "Mom is still against me doing that. The doctor asked her if he needed to give me a prescription and she said no."

Moms, I know you are screaming while reading this right now. But that was Isabella! Sure, despite her mothering issues, she was cool. But she was also confus-ING! From jump, she knew about Raheem and she kept that information from Mr. Rinaldi. She made it okay for Ange to get an abortion. Once again, she kept those facts from Mr. Rinaldi. But she wouldn't let Ange get on the pill. Yeah, I know why: because then she'd be admitting that Ange was having sex.

Somehow, Isabella must have erased the sex-abortion connection from her brain. It was probably the same eraser that disconnected her Catholicism from the abortion issue.

This was the stand Isabella was taking, but Ange could play her own hand. She didn't need permission to get on the pill. Planned Parenthood was a phone call away.

"I don't know. I'll see what Raheem says. I'll probably get on 'em. I don't want to go through this again."

Ange's voice sounded weak, as though she was on the verge of losing it.

"What's wrong, Ange?"

She cried, "Oh, Sheree. You didn't tell me I'd be so sad. I can't believe I did this. It was a baby. A little baby. My baby."

I had no answer, just open arms. Rocking her as she cried, I wouldn't allow myself to even go there. No way would I start thinking about my own dead baby, or I would probably start too.

WEEKS LATER

After having been stood up, I was finally cooled off enough to see Roc. Of course, he didn't come see me. Yeah, a part of me hoped he would track me down. But

93

I never put money on hope. Or wishin'. 'Cause neither would ever make me rich.

It was early afternoon when I walked to the Ice House. Taking me to the back where it was nice and cool, some man led me to Roc. There he was with that caramel complexion that we share, in his work suit, lifting ice bricks. Naturally, he was surprised to see me. You know the way he looks when he's tryin' not to smile? Well, that was the grin he quickly flashed at me. Then it was gone. After moving some loads into a colder room, he took me outside.

It was, like, ninety degrees. I wished we could have stayed inside the Ice House. But I wasn't gonna tell him that. I was just glad he looked somewhat happy to see me.

Wiping the sweat from his brow, he asked, "Your mom tell you I came by the other day?"

I wanted to answer, "Other day? That was three weeks ago," but instead I said, "Yeah. She said you'd be by the next morning. I waited for you."

Stroking his goatee, slowly nodding his head, Roc shuffled his feet. "Yeah, I was tryin' to make my way past. Nettie had me runnin' around the mall. Lil' Roc needed some new sneakers."

Walking over to the Ice House, I promised myself that I would keep my attitude in check. I didn't. As soon as Roc mentioned Nettie, something inside me changed. I cracked my Juicy Fruit, and my hands rested on my broad hips. My lips slowly went north. *I can't stand Nettie!* She tried to keep him from seein' me. He probably told her his plans and then she made up the story about Lil' Roc needing sneakers.

Trust me, there ain't nothin' Lil' Roc needs. He probably has a pair of Iversons, Jordans, Rocawear, and G-Units. Nettie keeps that seven-year-old up.

Swallowing my temper, searching for an even tone, I asked, "Well, why didn't you just pick me up and we all could have gone to the mall together?"

Avoiding my eyes, he said, "Nettie went with us."

Of course! I couldn't go 'cause Nettie went. *I can be nice to her!* Did he think I was gonna act up or something? C'mon, I'm not six years old!

Fighting to keep my voice and attitude in check, I said, "Well, I would have liked to have seen Lil' Roc. I haven't seen him in, like, a year."

Finally looking at me, he said, "Yeah, I know. He asks about you, too."

My hands left my hips and I couldn't help smiling. "He does?"

Lil' Roc may be spoiled, and have the wrong mother, but he's a cutie.

"Yeah. He asks me when it's just me and him,

though. I'll bring him by next time I come. A'ight. I gotta get back in here before the boss starts lookin' for me. Take care now." Roc patted my arm and left.

The door shut and once again Roc and I were separated. I couldn't help but feel jealous. Lil' Roc got time alone with Roc. What did I get? A five minute conversation about nothing, outside in the heat.

Lil' Roc got a daddy. He even called Roc Daddy. Not Roc, like I was programmed. Lil' Roc got a daddy who came home practically every night, a daddy who took him places, bought him things, taught him things—and one who probably tucked him in at night.

Even when I was a kid, I don't think Roc put me into bed. He never lived with us, He's always been someone who drops by every once in awhile. Never a set schedule. Mostly unannounced. Since he played disappearing acts, you never fronted like some moms—never made him out to be more than he was: a sperm donor, who occasionally gave you some money and me some time. "Wait until your dad comes home, finds out, whatever"; you never uttered that. Shoot, you and Mom Mom just handled your business.

After leaving the Ice House, I headed back toward home. One of Damon's boys drove past me walking and stopped to give me a lift. Although I was thankful for the lift, my mood was like the weather, boiling. I was itching for a fight. Someone to hit, tell off, curse out. Chris caught it all.

"Where's your boy been at? I haven't seen nor heard from him in a week! He's screenin' my calls. You tell him I said forget it! Don't call me. Don't come to my house or nothin'! I don't want nothin' to do with him no more. He's dead to me."

"Damn! Well hello to you too, Sheree. What's wrong with you?"

"Nothin! I'm sick of Damon! Sick of guys! Sick of it all! Just give him the message . . . please."

When Chris dropped me off, he didn't say if he would deliver my message. I never could tell with Chris. It probably depended on Damon's mood whether or not my words would be repeated.

Anyway, I was still in an ugly mood later that night, so I stayed home. It was the first Friday I hadn't gone out somewhere. I just wasn't in the mood to be bothered.

Solace and peace. Neither were in our house. Believe me, I searched, but you and Candy kept pestering me! It started with clothes. You were finally allowed to go back to Regal's. Wanting to look your best, my closet is where you and Candy shopped. Even when I had my headphones on, y'all didn't get the message, removing them from my ears, asking me if this looks okay? Does that? Giving me the 411 on Miss

97

Phyllis and Smoky. Who cares? But y'all couldn't get out of the door fast enough. I wanted to be alone. Wanted to sit in my room. Play some Mary J. I wanted, I needed, to think.

A slammed door. No thank-you for the outfits. No good-bye. But I'll take it. Y'all were finally gone. All night I sat in my bedroom. I didn't watch TV or answer the phone. It was just me, Mary J., and my thoughts.

I thought I was thinkin' about what I was gonna do, what's next, what I was gonna do after I graduated this year. But my mind kept taking me back to places I didn't want to go—to the past. I wondered if my future was somehow tied up in there.

Remember when I started high school? Some people had trouble going from the middle to the high school. I wasn't one of them, though. I automatically fit in. Hanging around older classmates was a natural progression for me. Besides, no one could intimidate me.

Not only wasn't the social adjustment a problem, but neither was the schoolwork. First trimester, I got my first and only A, three Bs, and two Cs—my best report card ever. And what did you say about it? Tryin' to remember? Let me refresh your memory. Nothing. You said nothing, Moms! Neither did Roc. Why?

Do you know how hard I worked to get those

grades? Studying every night—doing my homework and turning it in on time—that was hard!

In elementary school, the school psychologist convinced you I couldn't learn without taking those ghetto pills—Ritalin. The prescription and dose were frequently given and sold to poor children and their parents. Children labeled hyperactive. Some, like Candy's son, KK, legitimately were. Others, like myself, were active, but not overly active. What six-year-old isn't active? I just wasn't used to sitting still for a long time. But I was able to. And I could do it without drugs. But you fell for the doctor's lines—hook, line, and sinker. The ghetto pills slowed me down. Made thinking harder. The doctor said taking them would make learning easier. It didn't! Taking 'em just made it easier for the teacher, so maybe she should have taken them! Once I was on them, of course I would sit still—still as a log. The pills made me move and think like a robot. I was always two steps behind everyone else.

After a few years, I fooled all of y'all and just stopped taking those suckers. No one even noticed. That's when I really knew I didn't need 'em. I just needed to remember to stay seated in class, not bother the teacher, and raise my hand.

Pill-free, I continued to follow the classroom rules,

but I was never moved into smarter classes. Teachers often accused me of being disruptive. No one had warned me I shouldn't question the teacher. In "their" classroom, "their" school, "their" environment, "they" fronted to be the only authority. I never accepted my place as a submissive student.

Anyway, I saw the high school as a new start. It was full of teachers who didn't know me, who hadn't labeled me . . . disruptive . . . quick-tempered . . . not cooperative . . . talks too much . . . poor student . . . poor, and all those other adjectives teachers use. At the high school, I was able to escape all of that. I worked my butt off. I got good grades. Proved a stupid psychologist, and some teachers, wrong! I felt great. I had also proven something to myself: that I am smart; I'm not dumb.

And myself was the only one cheering. There wasn't a single applause elsewhere. When no one—not you, not Roc, or even any of my teachers—said anything to me, I quit. Yep, right then and there, I quit. I quit tryin'. Why bother? Y'all seemed to say more when I brought home Cs, Ds, and the occasional F.

Teachers: "Not working to ability."

You: "They're gonna put you out of school if you don't do better! Do you want to work at Mickey D's? That's where you're headin,' full-time job at Mickey D's."

Obviously, y'all couldn't motivate me. I discovered I didn't have to work hard to get just passing grades. Shoot, depending on the teacher, I just had to show up and I could count on a C. The teachers who required more than my presence got bare-bones work from me—just enough to get by.

The only place I was willing to work was on the track. It wasn't just because running came easy to me either. I loved track. Loved my coaches, too. They always believed in me.

Remember when I came home from my first big Saturday meet? I had won three medals! First in the one-hundred meters, third in the two-hundred meters, and our four-hundred relay team got a first place medal too. You smiled when I told you about my races. That made me feel so good. You said, "Ree Ree, I always knew you would be fast. Just like me. I ran when I was in school. I was real fast too. Couldn't no girls and some boys beat me. I always wondered if I would have gotten a running scholarship to go to college or something. But I had you. And that was the end of running for me."

Well, the first part of what you said made me feel good, anyway. The rest? Well, you know, Moms, I always feel bad when you tell me how you got pregnant and dropped out of school. Sometimes—most times—

you say it like it's my fault or something. Why? I didn't ask to be born! I didn't ask for this! I didn't ask for a part-time dad like Roc! I didn't even ask for you. You and Roc brought me here, so deal!

Okay, sorry, the ink is smudging. I'm done going down that side of memory lane. It hurts too much.

THREE DAYS LATER

Despite myself, I took Damon back. No begging. But a Damon-type apology was given. Basically, he told me he'd been busy lately and he padded my Fendi wallet. So what could I say? Plus, he promised to give me more of what I needed: time. I'm not foolin' myself into believing he'll dis his boyees, 'cause ain't no man ever gonna do that. But as long as he's spending a little more time with me and on me, that's cool. The first few days, he called me, like, every day. If I didn't see him, he called. The conversations were quick. Damon hates to talk long on the phone. But at least we talked. Once, he actually took me out. Red Lobster. It was just the two of us; his boyees didn't even tag along. I ordered the Ultimate Shrimp Platter. Damon got crab legs. Sitting beside him in the booth, I was beginning to think things were lookin' up for us.

"Baby girl? You know you're my number one,

right?" he asked while sipping a rum and coke.

Yeah, I knew that. It didn't make sense wishin' there wasn't a number two or three. Ain't that what you taught me, Moms? A man is gonna be a man. That means he's gonna creep no matter what. So I wasn't about to ruin our dinner with a losing argument. I nodded my head and ate my food. Later, I thanked him.

Not even four days later, the old Damon was back! I hadn't seen or heard from him, and I was on the phone with Austin complaining about it.

"Sheree, I'm tired of hearing about Damon."

"C'mon, Austin," I begged. "I need your help. What should I do?"

Austin sighed. "I told you umpteen times to cut him loose. He's just usin' you. What would I look like tellin' some girl they're my number one? Shouldn't you be his *only* one?"

"Aw, Austin! Damon was complimenting me. He was saying the others don't mean nothin'. All men cheat. And I ain't gots no problem with bein' number one. As long as him and those others give me my respect, I'm cool. I just want him to call more. Come over and not just to do it. To take me out again."

"Sheree, first of all, don't call Damon a man. Look,

my dad taught me and his dad taught him about being a man. None of it ever involved running women, or sticking your manhood into every P. I was taught the opposite. You find one good girl, who respects herself and you. Take care of her and cherish her. Don't allow anyone to disrespect her. My dad always says a real man doesn't need but one woman. The person who's frontin' to be a man, with lots of women on the side, doesn't know who he is yet—"

I interrupted. "Damon knows who he is."

"No, he doesn't. If he did, he wouldn't need two and three girls to help feed his ego. Sheree, think about it! Damon's twenty-two. Why does he only mess with young girls?"

"Austin, I ain't no young girl! He's only five years older than me, anyway. That's not much. Age ain't nothin' but a number."

"Yeah, five years is, if you think about what he should be doing—and that you're still in high school."

"My *last* year of high school. I thought you would understand and try to help me."

"I am helping you. If you want me to give you some girlie advice"—Austin began imitating a girl's voice—"talkin' about stick with him, girl, he gives you money; he's cute; he dresses nice, and all of that"—putting the base back in his voice, he continued—"then call one of your girlfriends! You basically told him you're cool with being his side piece as long you're number one. You've shown him he doesn't have to do jack, but maybe give you some money, and he gets all the booty he wants. So why would he change the rules and start calling and taking you out now?"

This time I was tempted to hang up on Austin. But I didn't. After all, I did call him laying my problems at his feet. I'm not sure why I continued to call him, though. Yeah, I liked him. But he also had this annoying way of getting under my skin.

See, Austin talked like he knew everything, but he was a young buck. What did he know about being a man? He didn't even have a girlfriend. He'd been here for a year and hadn't messed with one girl. I bet he was a virgin, too. Always talkin', sayin' exactly what was on his mind. He made me sick sometimes. What did he know about Damon? He didn't even know him.

I knew Damon. We'd been together for almost a year and a half. His mom raised him and his older brother, Darryl. They're only a year apart. Darryl is an officer in the marines, stationed somewhere in Iraq. I heard their mom was always praying and crying for him. She had CNN on all the time. Once, she caught a glimpse of his unit in some sandstorm or somethin'. Damon and Darryl didn't get along, though. Damon accused Darryl of selling out. And Darryl called Damon a bum, mostly because Damon didn't have a "real" job. Hustling and selling weed and rocks ain't workin', as far as Darryl is concerned.

But what Darryl didn't know, and nobody else knew, was that Damon wasn't gonna do that all his life. He said he was tryin' to get out of the game. He just had to make some more money—to buy a storefront, a few apartments, and a house. Once he did that, he was quittin' for good.

I doubted Damon would buy a storefront. I already told you about that pipe dream involving barbecue sauce. But I was sure he'd get his own house. He didn't want to live with his mom forever. And being his numero uno, he was gonna need me by his side. Right? I'd accept number one status for now. Nothing better was coming, so I might as well hold on to what I had— even if it was only a little bit.

Saving my breath, I didn't share all of that with Austin. He would never understand—never understand Damon or me. I think I understand us both.

Around noon the next day, I was on a road trip. Enough time had passed that Isabella finally allowed Ange to hang out again. So you know where we went?

Philly, yes. Point Breeze, no. Raheem and Russell were meeting us on South Street. We couldn't chill at Raheem's house because his mom was sleeping before going to work. Instead, we were meeting at this restaurant called John's on South Street.

"Ann-ge-la!" Lifting her into his arms, Raheem kissed her.

It was the first time the two had seen each other since . . . I knew Ange breathed for this man. But his excitement caught me off guard.

"Are you feeling okay, baby?" Raheem asked.

Ange nodded, burying her face into his shoulder. It was obvious she was holding back tears. Attempting to take the attention off of her, I asked, "Y'all hungry or what?"

Everyone was. Ange was able to focus on food as we added our names to the growing list of those waiting for a table. Between the tourists, lunchtime crowd, and general popularity of John's, we had more than an hour wait. We spent it sitting outside near the curb. Growing impatient, Ange thought a carriage ride would help time pass faster.

"You and Raheem go. I'll stay here in case they call our name."

There was no way I was riding in a carriage with Russell. Damon, definitely. Austin, probably. But

Russell? Nah! I was fine with just talking to him on the street. No need to be hugged up close. He was nice-looking and all—nice cleft in his chin, keeps a haircut. But he was too much like his boy: broke!

Like Raheem, Russell lived with his mom. But Russell didn't freeload. He had a little job working at the Boys & Girls Club, but all of his money went toward college. Russell went to Lincoln University. He was taking computers or something like that.

"Rah-sool, what's college like?"

"A big high school."

"For real?"

"Straight up. I always thought I couldn't wait to go to college. You know, escape the silly stuff from high school. And then I got there, and there's more drama than in high school! The best part about college, though, is the freedom."

"Freedom?" I looked at Russell intensely and asked, "What do you mean?"

"You don't have teachers or parents sweatin' you. The professors don't hunt you down if you miss their class. And there's no parents to ask you where you've been and when are you coming home."

"Oh, is that all? I got freedom now. I've always had that."

What I didn't have were any plans to go to college.

Actually, Moms, we never discussed what I would do next. I don't know what I want to do. Or be. After graduation, I can't see myself sittin' in any more boring classes, though. I guess I'll just get a job somewhere.

As soon as Ange and Raheem returned, our table was ready. We talked, ate, and left. The rest of the afternoon was spent going in and out of the unusual shops on South Street.

Everything was going well until Ange had a silly idea. She was craving something sweet. Okay, no problem. There was an ice cream shop up the street. However, Ange didn't want ice cream. She wanted a chocolate-chip cannoli. And not any cannoli either. It had to come from Marsala's, her aunt and uncle's sandwich shop and bakery. During the school year, Ange turned me on to Italian pastries. After tasting cannoli and tiramasu elsewhere, there's no denying that Marsala's makes the best. The ricotta melts in your mouth, it is so creamy. Although Marsala's was a quick three-block walk, I was uneasy about all of us going there. But Ange, who's used to getting her way, insisted.

"Angela." Short and fat, Uncle Louie welcomed Ange with a big hug and kiss.

"And Sheree." He pulled me into a bear hug too.

"Sit down. Let me get you something to eat. Your aunt is at the house; she'll be in later."

Suddenly, Uncle Louie's expression changed. He finally noticed our black six-foot companions. It was obvious that they were with us.

"Uncle Louie, this is my boyfriend, Raheem," Ange said, putting her hand through Raheem's arm.

The lines on Uncle Louie's face took a neutral position, making it difficult to read exactly what was running through his mind. Although he said hi, he didn't offer his hand, not even to Russell.

Why did Ange have to call him her boyfriend, anyway? She could have just said our friends, left it at that. Yeah, Uncle Louie probably wouldn't have believed her. But telling the truth left no possibility for doubt.

When we were seated in a booth, I asked Ange why she was so honest.

"Why not?" Ange asked me.

"'Cause you know he's gonna tell your dad. He's probably on the phone in the kitchen calling your aunt Carlita. And after she calls your nana, her sisters, and her other brother, she'll call your dad."

"I don't care anymore. What can he do?" Taking a forkful of cannoli, she asked, "Baby, didn't you say you didn't like sneaking around anymore?"

Raheem nodded. But who cared what he thought or wanted? He wasn't really sneakin' anyway. In Philly, they weren't incognito. They were and have always

110

been out in the open. Just not there, at Marsala's, or at Ange's house. Raheem also didn't have anything to lose.

As we were eating our cannoli and drinking cappuccino, Ange's aunt Carlita busted into the restaurant. Aunt Carlita is taller than Uncle Louie by a bouffant. Her brownish-red hair is teased high, and she has bangs, which hang in her face. If she updated her do, she'd be real pretty. Nobody told her big hair is out. Gone. Aunt Carlita's hair is so high that when she works in the kitchen she has to wear two hairnets to cover that mop.

The way Aunt Carlita ran into the restaurant and marched straight over to our table, it was clear that Uncle Louie had given her a heads-up.

"Angela, Sheree," Aunt Carlita said, offering hugs and Hollywood kisses. Then her eyes and perfectly waxed eyebrows rested on Raheem and Russell. "Who do we have here?"

No use lyin' now. Ange repeated her answer. Aunt Carlita, ever the actress, was better able to hide her feelings. She spoke and then proceeded to ask a string of questions.

"What's your last name? Where do you live? How old are you? Do you go to school? Work? How did you meet Angela? How long have you been seeing her?"

She took a breath. I thought it was over. But Aunt Carlita was just warming up. . . .

"Have you met my brother Darius and his wife, Isabella? Why not? Has Angela met your parents? Just your mom? Do you see your dad? Well, what does your mom say about you two? She doesn't say anything about it? She doesn't say anything about Angela's race? Her age? Nothing?"

Another breath . . .

"Tell me, do you only date white girls? You date everyone? Are you only seeing my niece? Do you treat her well? Keep your hands to yourself?"

Finally, the questions ended. Oddly enough, Raheem didn't seem to be uncomfortable about the matter. Aunt Carlita had her information, chatted a bit more, and then excused herself. A natural gossip, I was sure she rushed to pick up the telephone in the kitchen and give a report.

"That's just the beginning, baby. I told you my family is like that." Ange lightly kissed Raheem's cheek.

"Yeah, Aunt Carlita even questioned me." I laughed. "And I'm a friend. But she means well. I noticed they're all protective of each other that way."

"It's cool, Angela baby. I like her. She asks what's on her mind. I can respect that."

We finished eating, said our good-byes, and left

Marsala's. Although Ange and I were willing to hang out some more, Russell needed to be at work by six o'clock. Surprisingly, they took the bus back home. The Honda was our means.

When Ange dropped me off at home, I wished her luck. She was going to need it. It was just six o'clock. Still early, but there wasn't a doubt in my mind that Mr. Rinaldi was already home. He was probably sitting in the beige wing chair in the living room, sipping his Grand Marnier, fuming. If Isabella was home, she was probably trying to calm him down. She didn't tell him she already knew about Raheem—of that much I was sure.

What I wasn't sure of is why Ange always did things to push her dad's buttons. She knew he wouldn't allow this. He wouldn't approve of Raheem. He's black. He's twenty years old. He doesn't work. He doesn't go to school. He lives in the city. Mr. Rinaldi would reject it all. So why throw it in his face? Is Raheem really the one she wants to bring home to dinner? Why not keep everything undercover, to see where the relationship goes? But Ange wouldn't do that. She must get some type of sick pleasure watching the veins bulge in Mr. Rinaldi's neck. And she must enjoy listening to him yell and call her names.

Early the next morning, Ange called me.

"How did it go?" I groggily asked.

"Well, you know he was there when I got home. Sure, he can come home early to yell at me. Where is he usually? Anyway, he said I can't see Raheem anymore. He made me call him on the phone and break up with him. He even spoke to Raheem, telling him he's too old for me, threatening to call the police if we see each other. Then Daddy took the keys to my car!"

"Dag! All of that? What did Raheem say?"

"He listened. I called him back when Daddy left, and told him to forget about all of that. I'm not breaking up with him for real! He's all that I got. I'm done sneaking around too."

Tired and frustrated, I yawned. "Ange?"

"I mean it, Sheree! Daddy can't run my life. I'll be eighteen next year. The only thing he does is order me around. He orders my mom, too! He thinks we're just supposed to listen to him. But Tony? Tony can do whatever he wants. Flunk out of school, send him to another one. Total a car because he's drunk, buy a new one. Tony can do no wrong in Daddy's eyes. His girlfriend isn't Italian or Catholic, either. Yet Daddy never says anything about that."

What could I say? I knew what Ange was feelin'. Some call it sibling rivalry. Whatever. I felt the same way about Eric, Randy, and sometimes even Lil' Roc.

114

I'm the oldest, and Roc's only girl. But he doesn't pay me no mind. He's never been to one of my track meets. But Eric's football games? And Randy's baseball games? He's on the sidelines yelling. Both of their moms get along with Roc about the same as you do, Moms, so I can't even act like it was your attitude that kept him away. I can't help wondering if it had something to do with me.

Ange is actually lucky because she and Tony get along great. Her older brother spoiled her to death.

Me and Eric don't even like each other. I'm the oldest by three months and he hates that. When he was younger, he used to try to test me. It would be on one of those rare visits when Roc wanted to get all of his kids together at his mom's or current girlfriend's house. Eric would step to me about a toy, or his turn on the bike, and I'd have to kick his butt. And even though that butt kickin' was years ago, Eric still holds it against me.

Randy was okay. I think with time and without his mom's interference, we could have been friends. His mom? Randi? You're right; she's touched, but not by an angel, to name a boy after her like that. Well, Randi doesn't like any of Roc's kids. Like it's our fault Roc doesn't take care of his kids or regularly visit. That is, unless Randy has a bat in his hand, and then it's all good. I hear Roc goes to just about every one of Randy's home games.

As much as I like and love Lil' Roc, sometimes I wish he wasn't around. I wonder what it would be like if it was just me. You think then Roc would notice me? Would he visit more?

Since I had my own sibling issues, I couldn't offer Ange any advice there. But I tried to get her to let Raheem go. I told her this wasn't the move. Somehow I knew that if she continued seeing him, it would end in disaster. But Ange wasn't hearing me, so I changed the subject.

"So, how long are you going to be without a car?"

"I don't know. I'm grounded. He won't say how long. I'm supposed to stay in and around the house. No company. It feels like a jail already. Soon Mom will complain about me being around the house all the time, in her hair, in her space. Then Daddy will give me my keys back. I think I'll be driving to Philly by the weekend."

Three weeks later, Ange was still on lockdown. Isabella complained, but Mr. Rinaldi wouldn't let up. He was affecting my summer. I missed seein' Ange.

Shopping. Lunches. I missed my girl. As it was, I was seeing very little of Damon, so my days were spent inside watching the soaps, and nights at the courts or corner lookin' for him.

One morning, I was about to walk to the pike, to Heavenly Nails for an appointment. The silk wrap on my thumb needed to be repaired. It kept lifting. Just as I was about to leave, Damon came walking up the steps.

"Oh, so you remember where I live? Where have you been?" I questioned.

"Sheree, don't come at me like that. How many times I've got to tell you I ain't about drama? Now get over here and show me some love, baby girl."

"Oh, Boo." Although I was still a little salty, now that he was there, I didn't want him to leave. *Skip the appointment*.

Damon and I hung around the house all day. He was still there when you got home from work.

"Hi, Damon. Y'all spend the whole day on my couch? Sheree, you clean up the kitchen. Damon, you got a bag?"

As Damon gave you the little bit that he had, I learned why he stayed so long. It had nothing to do with me. He was laying low. Popo was in the hood. Word was some people were rounded up and taken in.

Y'all laughed and lit up his stash. When it was my turn, I passed it over to you. Both of y'all looked at me funny.

"What? I don't feel like it."

Some more laughter, 'cause that meant there was more for y'all. I walked out of the room and onto the porch. I didn't want a contact either.

When night finally fell, Damon dragged himself home. Several hours before, I'd grown tired of his company. Once I realized the true purpose of his visit, his welcome was worn on me. I was tired. Tired of him. And when you came home? It was like he wasn't my company anyway. You and he smoked. Later, your friend Rodney dropped by. Then all of y'all smoked, talked, drank, and ate. Would it have bothered you to include me in at least one of the conversations? Save your breath, Moms. I didn't expect you to really answer that.

Although it was dark, it was still early. Perfect time to go out! This girl named Beverly was having a party in her backyard. It sounded live. I could hear the music bangin' from the front stoop. Even though I knew Austin would be there and maybe even Jerome, too, I didn't feel like going. I was too tired. I wanted to go to sleep.

As I was walking up the steps, I glanced at you and

118

Rodney sitting on the couch. Moms, what do you see in him? His gear—white linen pants with an orange shirt—is okay. I'll give him that—he can dress. And he's not ugly. But there's something about him that looks dirty. Like if you look past his flashy clothes, you'll find dirty underwear. Or that he only lotions the body parts people can see. I can't put my finger on it. But I know you could do and have done better.

Moms, for thirty-two, you still look good. Your breasts, as big as they are, don't sag. You got just the right amount of junk in your trunk. And wrinkles? The only line on your face is that scar from where some chick sliced you in the face a few years ago. So, Brown Betty (remember Mom Mom called you that, talkin' about your beautiful brown skin?), you still got it goin' on! So what do you see in Rodney? What do you see in all of them that make their way to our house?

Time—that's what I had been askin' Damon for. After spending nearly twelve hours with me the other day, once again he was a ghost. Knowing him, he probably felt he put enough time in. For three days, I didn't see him or his car. He wasn't locked up or I would have heard. And his cell phone? Temporarily out of service.

Tired of kickin' it around the house, I walked to the basketball courts. Something was gnawing at me. I didn't know what it was, but I just had a sinking feeling something bad was about to happen. So why did I still go? What else was there to do?

As soon as I walked through the playground gates, I saw him. And I saw her. Damon and Ushama.

Ushama. Yeah, that's her crazy-ass name. Who knows what her mom was smokin', naming her that. Well, Ushama is some big-lipped, light skin chick who lives over the way. She's a junior and a definite around-the-way girl, if you catch my drift. She was also up in Damon's face. The way she was carryin' it, there was no question in my mind that they were together.

I saw them, but they didn't see me. They were too busy talkin'. But everybody else was busy watchin' the three of us. Crackin' my gum like crazy, I strolled over to them.

"Damon. Can I holla at you for a minute?"

They both jumped. She tried to play it off. He looked surprised to see me. I don't know why, though; it was *my* side of town.

"Oh, Sheree," he said casually.

"No. Damon's with me right now. He'll have to holla at you later," Ushama barked.

I got in her face. "Am I talkin' to you? Damon, you better set her straight. Bring her into my hood and try to jump bad? I don't think so."

The grittin' began.

Damon knew. He could try to front and act cool if he wanted, but he knew Ushama's hair would be all over the playground. Gently grabbing my arm, Damon took me a few feet away.

"What's up, Sheree?"

"Don't what's-up me. How you gonna bring that tramp here? How you doin' that to me?" I struggled to remain cool, but my voice, like my gum, was cracking.

"Look, calm down. You've always known I have plenty of friends. No rings, no attachments."

"Your 'friends' were never in my face before! How'd you like me to bring somebody up here, at the courts? 'Cause I ain't got any rings either!"

"Look, you know what's up. Don't be bringing anybody up here. They'll go home hurt. You know you're mine." He changed his attitude. "Besides, she don't mean nothin' to me. We're just talkin'; it ain't nothin', baby girl."

Not falling for the "baby girl," or his attempts to smooth things over, I made bold demands. "Then tell her to leave."

"Now, Sheree, how am I gonna make her leave? Look here"—he moved closer to me—"why don't you go home and I'll be by in a few?"

Just as I was about to stand up to Damon and tell him hell no, Ushama busted into our conversation. This trick is too bold.

"Damon? Why are you still talkin' to her?" Ushama asked.

My patience was wearing.

Firmly I said, "Uganda, this is between me and Damon."

"It's Ushama." Rolling her eyes, she added, "And anything you say to my man you can say to me."

My patience, gone! Dag, no matter how hard I'd try to change, someone would test me. After getting into it with that girl Lettica Morgan the last year, I promised myself I wouldn't fight no more. Especially over a man. When do they ever fight over or for us? Once we made up, I learned a lot from Lettica. She had all the black girls at the school getting along. We were thinkin' about unity, sisterhood, and stuff like that. It wasn't as corny as it sounds either. Or phony. A lot of us just changed our attitudes, dropped our beefs. Even if we didn't like somebody, we were all tryin' to respect one another. Name-calling, back-stabbing, fighting, wasn't the way. But this Ushama

122

and her mighty mouth was just callin' me—callin' me to kick her ass. Quickly, I thought it over. Kick her ass and maintain my street rep. Or walk away. I knew I should walk away. Ushama wasn't worth me breakin' a nail or getting my white minidress dirty. But you never taught me to walk away, so why should I then? If I walked away, Ushama and everybody there would think I was scared. No way!

Just as I snatched my gold big-hooped, name-plated earrings off, Damon snatched Ushama.

"C'mon, Ushama, you got to go," Damon said.

"Go? Nah, what's she gonna do? I ain't scared of Sheree."

I swung at her but Damon moved her away too fast. Her mouth was still running, but I couldn't understand a word. Damon was covering those big lips. Then he told her to shut up, and just like a dog, she obeyed. I saw her trying to look around inconspicuously. Once she was silenced, Damon turned on me.

"How you gonna be fighting? You know you shouldn't be doing this now. I told you to go home."

Damon obviously got his dog confused with the lady! He wasn't my master, so I wasn't leaving. I was angry—angry at Damon for bringing her here, the courts, of all places! And angry at him for talkin' to me like that in front of everybody. I was also angry at

Ushama with her big mouth. I was angry at them, but I think I was even angrier with myself. Yeah, he didn't show me any respect. Ushama, with her trash-talkin' self didn't give me none either. And me? I showed out for nothing. Jeopardizing . . . I should have just kept my butt home.

I didn't even try to save face by staying at the courts. After Damon and Ushama left, I bounced too. People were already talkin'. I could tell. Only one person was brazen enough to invade my furious state. Who else would be so daring but Austin? As I was walking home, he ran up to me.

"Sheree, what was all that for?"

"Austin, don't start with me. I'm not in the mood, all right? I was just trying to talk to Damon and she was the one gettin' loud. Not showing me any respect. Damon was wrong too, bringing her up in here."

"So you were going to fight her over him?"

"No. She was talkin' smack. If she would have given me my respect, I wouldn't have any beef with her."

"So it's a respect thing?"

"Yeah."

"Oh, she's supposed to respect you? Even though you don't even respect yourself enough to walk away from Damon and her?"

I stopped walking and looked at Austin and his

freshly done cornrows. He really is a nice-looking guy.

"Austin, why do you care?"

"I just wonder why you *don't* care."

With my hand on my hip, I cracked my gum and shook my head. I understood.

"Austin? You say you don't wanna get with me, but you're always questioning me like this. You know I could pull any of these guys on the corner right now, like that." I snapped my fingers. "What's up with you? Be real."

Austin moved real close to me. I thought he was about to kiss me so I stopped crackin' my gum and moved it to one side of my mouth. As he leaned in, I closed my eyes and tilted my head up toward him.

"Once again, Sheree . . ." Hearing his low voice, I quickly opened my eyes, adjusted my head, and hoped he didn't see that. Austin continued whispering, "Once again, Sheree, it's about respect." Then Austin walked back toward the courts.

Just once, thinking there might be a chance, I made a fool of myself. Running after him, I yelled, "What do you mean? I respect you."

He stopped and looked deep into my eyes.

"Yeah. No doubt. No doubt, you respect me. For some reason, you even respect Damon. But you don't respect yourself. Or you wouldn't even be lookin' at those bums on the corner. You think the answer to your problems can be solved between your legs. Your problem *is* what's between your legs! I'd like you more if you respected that."

I don't know which one of us stepped first, but we each went in separate directions. Austin's words, his actions, all of it, confused me. Finally I made it home. Shutting Austin, Damon, Ushama—everyone—off, I walked upstairs, locked my door, and went to sleep.

I was still in a fog when Ange called late the next morning. Her parents had left to go gambling in Atlantic City, and Ange found the keys to her car, refusing to be a prisoner on such a beautiful, sunny day.

My schedule? Wide open. She picked me up and we headed to Philly. Only, Ange couldn't reach Raheem on his cell. When she called his house, his mom said he wasn't there.

I asked, "So what are we gonna do now?"

"Let's go down South Street. We'll stay away from Marsala's, though. I want to get a hat at that hat shop on the corner."

So South Street it was. It was already packed. Parking spaces were hard to find, forcing us to park, like, six blocks over.

Our first stop was the hat store, where Ange bought a fly linen fedora. It was tight! And she looked too cute in it. After leaving umpteen messages on Raheem's cell, he still hadn't hit her back yet.

"Are you hungry?"

I nodded my head.

"Let's get something to eat."

The first place we stopped at was too crowded, the wait too long. On a nice day like this one, I had a feeling all of the restaurants would be crowded. A street vendor would be our best bet at fast food, but I didn't feel like standing to eat.

"Okay. Let's walk to Jim's, then. We just have to eat soon. I didn't have any breakfast," Ange said.

You know, Moms, Ange cracks me up. She was always talkin' about breakfast. If she missed breakfast, she acted like it was the end of the world. Flaws aside, Isabella did pass on some motherly advice about nutrition. She taught—rather, drilled into—Ange that breakfast was the most important meal of the day. Ange assumed the message was universal. Although she tried to hide the change in her voice, I could tell she was shocked when I informed her that I hardly ever ate breakfast, especially on school mornings. On the weekends when I'd have time, I'd usually fix something. The problem was, in our house, if there was cereal, there was no milk. And if there was milk, no good cereals. Breakfast was a routine we just didn't have in our house.

Anyway, we continued walking up the street with Ange still complaining about missin' breakfast. It was almost one o' clock, I was about to kindly tell her to shut up and get over it, when she started getting excited.

"What?" I demanded.

"Look!" She pointed. "Isn't that Raheem?"

"Where?" I squinted, eyes competing with the sun's rays.

"Sitting at the table inside Jim's?"

I looked over. Yep, it was him! He was with some girl. Although her back was to us, we could see enough to know that although she was black, she wasn't a cousin—unless they were kissin' cousins.

Ange dodged a few cars as she sprinted across the street. I was several strides behind, definitely winded. As Ange loudly burst into the restaurant, Raheem looked her way. Knowing somethin' was about to go down, Raheem must have tried to warn girlfriend. She snapped her head around just as Ange and I approached.

I knew I had seen girlfriend's face before, but my mind couldn't remember where.

At first, Raheem tried to play the rapper Fabolous

role. Someone should have clued Ange in, because she didn't know she was supposed to be the shorty on the side!

Then it came to me—girlfriend was the chick who was at Raheem's party at the beginning of the summer. She was back at the house when Ange and I went there while waiting for Mr. Rinaldi to show up with the tow truck. Her friend, the mocha girl, was on Russell.

Ange's mind must have taken the same trip down the lane. She said, "I remember you. How long has he been seeing you?"

All the girl had to do was answer. Ange was coming to her straight, woman to woman. But no, this chick rudely demanded, "Didn't you get the hint to stay away from him?"

I got her message. This time I was determined to walk away, taking Ange with me. "C'mon, Ange. Let's go," I said.

Ange didn't move. "What do you mean? What hint? Raheem never told me about you."

The chick rolled her eyes and applied even more sass. "Your car?" she asked as she boldly put on burgundy lipstick.

Whatever girlfriend was drinkin', she was wearin', as Ange threw the girl's drink in her face. Ange was reachin' for the water glass when I tried to pull her away. The girl, who had so much to say before, was now yellin' about her hair. Apparently she had just gotten it done. Raheem tried to get the girl, whose name turned out to be Nadine, to chill. But you know, even if they have a relaxer, ain't no sista gonna relax with their sixty-dollar hairstyle drippin' wet. So Nadine was talkin' boo-coo junk.

I kept trying to get Ange to move, but she kept screaming at Raheem. "How could you do this to me? You said you loved me." Then she screamed some more at Nadine. "You whore! You slashed my tires!" People who were eating stopped and stared. Ange was loud—not just in Jim's; her voice must have carried outside, too, 'cause hearing a commotion, people walking on the street stopped and looked inside the restaurant. The only person moving? The cop who arrested us all.

The four of us were taken to some type of community policing outpost. Not the roundhouse, but close enough. Once again, anger was filling my mood. I didn't want a record or fine. I was pissed! Pissed at Raheem, pissed at Nadine, and pissed at Ange for causing this interrogation.

After Sergeant Hill got the particulars, she gave us some good and bad news. We weren't under arrest. We weren't being charged with anything either. However, the manager at Jim's was banning us from his restaurant for one year. No problem. Somehow, I didn't see myself coming to South Philly that often anymore anyway.

The bad news? Since we weren't eighteen, Sergeant Hill wouldn't allow Ange and me to just leave. Raheem and Nadine, who were both adults in the eyes of the law, were free to go. But mine and Ange's parents had to be called. That's when Ange started boo-hooing. She thought—and I hoped—her tears would save us. After all, we had our own transportation home. No such luck. Sergeant Hill said she couldn't let us leave on our own—something about liability.

So for the second time this summer, Ange bit the bullet, making the call. From what I understood, Mr. Rinaldi was doing well at the poker table. Isabella was happily shopping at the Gucci store. Neither was pleased about being interrupted or inconvenienced. Mr. Rinaldi even spoke to Sergeant Hill on the phone, giving her permission to send Ange home. No can do.

While we waited, Sergeant Hill talked to us. If she were our mother, it would have been more along the lines of a lecture. Since she wasn't, we actually listened.

"What is it with you girls today? You know, I see girls like you, Angela and Sheree, all of the time. And it's always because they're fighting over some guy. You know what? I have yet to find one of their guys that's worth it. Your friend? Raheem? He's twenty years old and he doesn't go to school or have a job. What does that tell you about him? You two seem like smart girls. You're seniors, right? What are you going to do when you graduate? Are you going to college? Or do you plan to spend the rest of your life chasing guys like him around?"

We shook our heads. Ange explained how she wanted to open a spa and become a masseuse. As you know, Moms, I didn't have any plans yet. I was taking things as they came. However, Sergeant Hill tried to encourage me to come up with something. Some type of plan, some course of action.

"Well, Sheree, think about what you like to do. There are a lot of people in college who don't have a major. They often discover what they want to do when they're at college. Then again, college isn't for everyone either. There are also business, computer, art, technical, and beauty schools. You can study culinary arts and how to become a chef, computers and how to troubleshoot and fix problems, carpentry and construction—there are so many fields to choose from. And there's the service and the peace corps. Now is when you ladies should be thinking about your future. Start planning. Set some goals and go for them.

"You know people say it all the time, but I'm not sure you young people believe it: You really can be anything you want to be. But you've got to put your mind to it. And you've got to work to get it. Nothing comes easy.

"And I'll tell you, if you don't have an education or some type of skill, you're not going to make it out here, not in these times. When I was your age, people could graduate from high school and get a job with just their high school diploma. I'm talking about a good blue-collar union job, making good money. Today, those jobs aren't just hard to come by because some of those same factories have moved out of Philly, even out of the United States. But also because those companies that are still around have people with college degrees applying for them too. So you see, ladies, you have to be prepared. You both seem intelligent. Don't sell yourselves short. Okay?"

When Sergeant Hill was done talking, she got up

and went back to her desk. For some reason, her talk saddened me. No one had ever talked to me like that before, so serious, but also so sincere. She called me smart and intelligent. I've been called pretty dozens of times. But smart and intelligent?

I glanced at Ange. She seemed to be touched too. Looking at her sad face, my anger dissolved. Finally, I whispered to her, "Ange, why are we here?"

"Here? Or in Philly?" she asked me.

"In Philly. Why did we come? Your dad is going to kill you."

"Yeah, I know. He'll take the keys again. Or maybe he'll sell my car this time. But you know what, Sheree? I don't even care anymore. I had to see Raheem. Lately, he had been acting funny, kind of like he didn't want to be bothered anymore. I had to see him, to find out what was going on, why he was treating me differently."

"Yeah, but was seein' Raheem worth losing your car?"

With no hesitation, Ange answered, "Yep. I know I sound crazy, after all of this, but I love him. I still do. And I know he loves me too. I know that. . . . He has to. I was just pregnant with his baby. He has to, Sheree, because no one else does." Ange began crying.

Since she was talking so loudly, I was sure Sergeant

Hill was dippin' in our conversation. However, she didn't comment. Sergeant Hill gave us our space as she continued to do her paperwork. As the day wore on, I think she read our minds, or heard our stomachs. My stomach was queasy and my body was feeling faint when Sergeant Hill offered us some food—sandwiches, chips, and sodas.

Nearly three hours later, Mr. Rinaldi and Isabella arrived. I couldn't tell who they were madder at, Ange and me, or Sergeant Hill.

I kept trying to reach you and even Roc, but y'all weren't anywhere to be found. Fortunately Mr. Rinaldi was able to convince Sergeant Hill to let me leave with them. I think she understood the Rinaldis were my only means of getting home.

Before we left, Sergeant Hill gave us a stern warning. She didn't want to see us in trouble again. She reminded us of our ban at Jim's. Then she suggested we write the manager a letter, apologizing for our behavior.

Out of respect for Sergeant Hill, I didn't say it. But I was thinking, *What do I have to apologize for?* I was—what do they always say on the news?—an innocent bystander.

But I, along with Ange, nodded my head and made promises. We even gave her a hug good-bye. I was going to miss her.

When we hit the pavement, Mr. Rinaldi's voice hit the clouds. I thought the sergeant was going to come out and arrest us again. Naturally, Mr. Rinaldi wanted explanations.

What were we doing there? Did Ange remember she's on punishment? Who were we fighting? Didn't he tell her to leave that *Rahim* alone? Didn't she know only an *uccello* could cause two women to fight? Did she lose hold of her senses? *Disgrazia!* Why can't she just listen? Why can't she just be a good girl like everyone else's daughter? What is he going to do with her?

People on the street watched but politely kept moving. Since Mr. Rinaldi wasn't yelling at me, I kept stealing looks at Ange's face. I wanted to see if she was embarrassed. How she could stand being yelled at like this. But as Mr. Rinaldi yelled, asked her questions, and called her names in Italian, Ange looked . . . alive? She should have looked beaten, defeated, humiliated even. He was putting her bidness on the sidewalk, in front of, oh, give or take, twenty, thirty people. But Ange looked at her dad with such love in her eyes. Yes . . . love! After a while, I stopped glancing and just ignorantly stared at her. I couldn't help it.

Isabella couldn't help herself either. However, instead of staring at Ange or Mr. Rinaldi, she was observing the people who were looking at them. She

136

was obviously embarrassed, her face growing redder by the minute. But the more Isabella attempted to shush Mr. Rinaldi, the louder he yelled. Giving up, Isabella walked a few feet away, creating enough distance so there wouldn't be any mistaking that she wasn't with us. Standing so far away, she looked like the other casual observers, nosily in our business. Perhaps I should have joined Isabella, but I couldn't move. My feet stayed planted, and so did my eyes—planted on Ange. Just as she was mesmerized with Mr. Rinaldi, I became so with her. Then finally I got it! My lightbulb moment! Why didn't I see it all before? Why did I bother questioning Ange? The answers were so clear to me now.

Standing there watching Ange's face, I finally understood. Her eyes, her expression, all of it told me the deal. Of course . . . this—stealing the car keys, getting caught, telling her relatives she was goin' with Raheem—was worth it. How couldn't it be? To anyone else it might not be, because who wants to give up a car? I wouldn't even part with a hoopdie if I had one. But a 2002 Honda, no way! But to Ange, yes. Yes! It was worth it! Because Mr. Rinaldi was finally paying attention to her. He was looking at Ange. Right in her eyes, too. I'm willing to bet she didn't even hear what he was really saying. He practically called her a whore.

The sound of his voice, despite the anger, was enough. It was enough for Ange because she knows in her heart that's all she's ever going to get from him.

That day I looked at my friend a little bit differently. I knew we had a lot in common. Deep down, I wondered if we shared this too.

Driving me home in Ange's car, Isabella raced down the expressway. Mr. Rinaldi and Ange were in his Benz. They were alone. My prayer was that Ange would open up and tell him how she felt. That music, more yelling, or awkward silences wouldn't be the only sound in his car.

It wasn't silent in the Honda. Between the loud music, Isabella asked me a few questions. She wanted to hear my side about what happened at Jim's. I filled her in. Wanting peace in her home, Isabella hoped Ange wouldn't be rebellious enough to stay with Raheem. "He appeared to be too much trouble," Isabella said. I laughed softly and wondered, *What guys aren't trouble?*

Dropping me off, Isabella waited until I was inside the house before pulling away. Home sweet home? Hardly! The smell met me at the door. Choking my throat, burning my eyes, the killer was killin' me.

"Hey, Ree Ree, baby. This is Nate. Nate, this is Sheree, my daughter."

Nate: Bald-headed and rocking a long beard like a Sunni Muslim, he was sprawled on our couch, sitting like he owned the place, with a fat cigar blunt in his hand.

You, dressed in your "company's over" short silk peach bathrobe, were sitting entangled with Nate. He was the reason you didn't answer the phone or your cell?

I heard him say, "What's up." But I was suddenly tired—tired from the events of the day; tired of Nates, Rodneys, and all others; tired of smelling weed; tired of you; tired of living like this! A grunt was my reply. Rolling my eyes? My way of welcoming your newest friend.

Obviously, I wasn't thinkin'. Because that type of greeting didn't go over too well with you. Taking the steps two at a time, you were following me up the stairs.

"I don't know what the hell your problem is. But this is *my* house! You are to speak to my company and act like you have some damn sense. You hear me? I'm the adult. You understand me? When you pay some bills up in here, then you can say somethin'. Until then, this is *my* house. If you don't like it, or my company, take your ass out and leave!"

After you walked out, slamming my bedroom

door, I locked it behind you. Once you were gone, I lay on my bed and thought about everything you said. Thinking was causing my head to hurt. So I turned the radio on to the "Quiet Storm." Music usually shuts my brain, but on this night, it opened my heart. I fell asleep listening to one of your favorite old songs. "Wildflower" by New Birth. The singer was saying something about being someone's bridge over troubled water.

The next morning I showered and dressed early. I didn't bother to touch the handle of your closed door. No doubt Nate was still there. Silently, I left the house. I knew what I had to cross. I just hoped he wanted to be my bridge. . . .

"Oh, it's you. It's a little early to be knockin' on people's doors. Didn't your mother teach your wild behind not to bother people before noon on Sundays?"

Remembering what I needed, I kept my wisecrack to myself. Yeah, I wanted to git with her. Git right up in her old, haggard-lookin' face. But doin' so wouldn't help me. And help was what I needed. So instead, as cheerfully as I could, I said, "Good morning, Nettie. I know it's early, but I need to see Roc. Can I see him, please?"

Rolling her eyes, she said, "What for? Whatchu want this time?"

Why does everything have to be so hard? Through a forced smile and a voice that didn't even have a dash of sass, I replied, "I don't want anything. I just *need* to talk to him. Is he home?"

Still blocking the door, "Of course he's here! He doesn't sleep all over town like some of the tramps he used to associate with." Narrowing her eyes, she added, "Roc knows where home is."

Moms, I had to let the tramp comment slide. My mission was much too important to get caught in a war of words with her. As it was, I was begging—begging to see my dad. I knew she had the power. And she knew I knew. My words, my body language, had to be kind and deliberate. If any part of me appeared to be challenging her conjured-up authority, then she wouldn't let me see him. Yes, she'd done this before.

The first time was three years ago. I was fourteen—not a little girl, but not the woman she came at me as either. Without calling first, Tameka and I went to his apartment, hoping Roc would give me some spending money for Great Adventure. Zion Baptist Church was taking its youth group there, and kids in the neighborhood could go too. I was all excited because you paid the forty dollars for my bus seat and ticket. Mom Mom took me shopping to get a fly short set. All I needed was some spending money. Just a little—no need for anyone to break open the bank.

After ringing the doorbell four times, we were about to walk away.

"Um, should have known it was you. Ringing somebody's doorbell four times like that. Don't you have no home training?" Nettie barked.

Barking right back, swiveling my neck, I answered, "Yeah, I do." I tried to walk past her and into the apartment, but she put her hands across the open door. Blocking my path.

"Oh, no you don't. You don't just come up in here any time you feel like it! This isn't your home." Nettie stared hard at me.

I met her stare. Tried putting my own icy flavor on it, but I couldn't hold my eyes that long. For one, I could feel Tameka eyeballing us both. Second, I wasn't used to staring down an adult like that. My eyes looked away first. Looking satisfied, Nettie demanded to know what I wanted. Feeling helpless, wondering why Roc didn't come to the door and stop her, I explained my intentions.

"Well, Roc's busy. He's playin' with his son. He don't have no extra money right now anyway. So you can get goin' now." Blowing cigarette smoke out her mouth, she added more toxicity to her insult. "Next time, call first. Don't just drop by here!" Then she slammed the door in my face. As Tameka stood there waiting for my next move, I willed myself together. I told myself to act tough, play it off. No one in our neighborhood had seen me cry. Tameka wouldn't be the first. What was welling inside of me had to stay there; it surfacing would cost me major cool points. As I fought to collect myself, Tameka and I walked home, penniless.

On the way we bumped into this guy named Varrick, who everybody called V. He had been tryin' to talk to me for a few weeks, but there wasn't room on my dance card. I was juggling a few others. However, I found out he wasn't just talkin' big; he had some bucks. So on that sorry day, I pushed the others aside, promising V it would be me and him at Great Adventure, sitting on the bus, enjoying the rides together. He'd have all of my time if he'd spend the dimes. He agreed. It was my first time squeezing a guy.

When I got home, you asked if I had some spending money and I was honest. I told you yes. Regurgitating Nettie's words would require me to relive it. So I never told you how she treated me that day, or any of the other times she hung up on me, or wouldn't let me even see Roc. Since that day, I planned to prove something to Nettie. I vowed that I would never ask Roc for anything. Money? No. Hugs? No. Nothing!

However, time and time again, Roc has proven that promises can be broken. So I broke mine, figuring I didn't have to prove nothing to Nettie anyway. There I was, three years later, making the same attempts to see him. And there she was in pink curlers about to deny me.

Again, sounding as sweet and patient as I could, I begged, "Can I please talk to Roc for a second? It's important."

Gritting her teeth, which matched her lemony skin, Nettie finally told me to hold on, and she shut the door. Yes, she made me wait in the hall, like I'm a pizza delivery person or somethin'! And that right there was just IG-NO-RANT! The whole thing! Telling me it's too early to knock on my own dad's door? And then leaving me in the hall of their apartment building? Perhaps I shouldn't have tried killing her with kindness; I should have just killed her!

By the time Roc came out into the hall, I was breathing fire. Word for word, I repeated what Nettie said and how she said it. Roc looked at me with those deep, dark eyes. I told him that was messed up. He looked away, then said, "Well, it is early. Nettie's not a morning person, that's all."

For some dumb reason, I was expecting Roc to agree with me. Don't ask me why, because he never stuck up for me in his life. To see where his allegiance lay, all I had to do was look at him. He was standing in the hall wearing pajama pants, talkin' to me. It's his apartment! So expecting him to man-up was wishful thinkin'. And you know how I feel about that.

As we stood in that narrow hall, I realized I was dreaming. Roc wasn't my Golden Gate. My Brooklyn. Heck, he wasn't even my Walt Whitman. He was more like that nursery school rhyme I learned at day care: London Bridge. I nixed my plans. Forget telling him; he couldn't help me anyway.

Looking a little disturbed, Roc asked, "What's up, Sheree? What do you want?"

Desperately holding in everything that I was feeling, keeping it in check, I answered, "Nothing. I just stopped by to see you. I was hoping I could see Lil' Roc, too."

Barely looking at me, he answered, "Well, he's looking at cartoons right now." Then he started stammering, looking around the hall. "And you know? Well, you know Nettie. Why don't you come back later? Give me a chance to talk with Nettie about that." Grabbing my hands, he added, "Here. Here's some money; buy yourself something."

He always thinks I want money from him. All men do. Why? I guess giving me that is easier than giving me what I really want or need. So yeah, I grabbed the twenty-dollar bill. I'm no fool! I don't know what he thought I could buy with it, though. But is he really that stupid? Why couldn't he just look at me and see? Doesn't he see me? Does he know me? I didn't even thank him; that was guilt money. He knew Nettie was wrong. More importantly, I sensed that he knew he was too. But since he didn't own up to it, I hated him.

Walking back to your house, I thought about how I couldn't even call it home no more. It was more like a rooming house. Strange people comin' and goin' all the time. It wasn't the type of place I should have been in then. It wasn't home.

Do you know what makes a home? From the *Cosby Show* reruns I learned about home. Home is where I should feel safe and loved, a place where I know someone has my back, not where I have to lock doors all the time. No, Moms, that wasn't home. I don't know if it *ever* was. Maybe Kevin stole that secure feeling from me. Perhaps I've been searching for someone to replace it.

I can't help but wonder if there ever was a time when I was your first and only concern. Did my needs ever come before yours? Did you know my cry?

Can you hear it now?

When I walked into the house, it was still asleep. I could tell you hadn't been downstairs yet. Quietly, I went back to my room and did what I had to do.

I remember back when Mom Mom moved out. Oh, how I cried, while you tried to explain to me that one house isn't ever big enough for two women. As I packed, I held on to that thought. Lots of things raced through my head as I was flooded with memories from my childhood to the present. But you know which thought haunted me the most? I wondered if I would be different.

I needed it so bad. But once I had it, would I know how to give it back? Was I capable . . . of love?

Soul-searching questions that only time can really answer. I just pray that it won't be in a letter from my daughter or son. I hope that I'll love them enough to see them—really see them. See that their titties are getting rounder, clothes getting tighter, and face getting fatter. I pray that I'll know that my baby is about to have a baby. And my knowing won't be discovered in a long letter like this one. My prayer is that I'll see it with my eyes, feel it in my heart and just know—know that my baby is in pain. Know that four months ago, back in May, I made a foolish decision—one that it is too late to take back now, one that has me terrified, and excited, too.

This pain I'm in hasn't just been the past three months either. Only recently, I realized that I've been struggling for a long time. Searching. Searching for someone to love me. Timmy, Bilal, Kareem, Doug, Damon—they couldn't find my heart. Heck, they didn't even try to look for it. They didn't have to. Finally, understanding Austin's words, I see that I made it too easy for them. Giving them all parts of me, sacred parts, and not demanding or even expecting them to unlock what was hidden inside. Money filled my dowry. Nothing filled my heart.

At home, "love," like "wildflowers," was treated like a curse word. No one to teach me about it. You didn't or couldn't. Roc didn't. Damon? The baby's daddy? Yeah, he knows. He's not too happy either. But what does he know about love? I don't think he knows how to love anyone but himself. But I think once it's born, he'll come around. So what choice do I have?

None. I've got to find out—find out if I am capable, find out if I can give and receive, too. Moms, I have to keep this one. It's all I have. And I'm gonna do it right, too. As soon as I found out, I stopped drinkin' and getting high. I'm trying to quit smoking, but that's so hard right now. (Those Newports be calling me, taking the edge off.)

The other day I think I felt it move inside of me. It was so quick. I haven't felt anything since then, though. So maybe it's too early for kickin', but it's coming. It's coming! This is real. One minute, I cry to myself wondering what I have done. Then the next, I think of how this is gonna change things for the better, give me what I need.

I hope it's a girl too. A pretty little girl with good hair. I'll put her in pretty dresses and stuff. Moms, she's never gonna see me get high! I'm not gonna let her smoke weed anyway. I'm'a cook dinner every night, breakfast every morning. Help her with her schoolwork, 'cause she's gonna be smart. And strange men? Not around my daughter! I won't need Damon or anybody else, because I'll have her. She's all I'll need. Since there won't be any men comin' and goin', there won't be any need for locked doors. I'm'a take care of her. Or him. Whoever is inside of me. Take care like a mom is supposed to do. Finally, I'm gonna have someone who loves me.

You and Mom Mom always talkin' about flowers. Wildflowers. Well, this is my flower . . . a rose. A rose, which I'll water, nourish, and help to grow. Grow slowly. And grow with all of my love. 'Cause I know there's love inside of me. There's got to be; my heart can't stay padlocked forever. I need to love. More than that, I need someone to love me back.

Take care, Moms!
Much love,
Sheree

Dear Ree Ree,

Thank you for finally writing me and letting me know where you are. I was worried.

The morning you left I woke up, saw your door was open, and walked into your room. Although your posters were still on the walls, teddy bears in the same corner of the floor, something was missing.

Yes, I could feel it. As your mother I could feel that your presence was somehow gone, not just temporarily, like you had gone to the store or something, but permanently. When I looked in your closet, I thought a few things were missing, but my suspicions weren't confirmed until I opened your panty drawer and it was empty and your cash was gone. (Yes, I've always known where you hide your money.)

As reality slapped me in the face, panic set in.

Where were you? Why did you leave? Were you okay? I tore your bedroom upside down, looking for clues to answer all my damn questions. Nate heard me and came into your room. But he didn't belong in there, did he? When I looked at him, I realized he didn't belong in our house, our home, either.

"Just go!" I snapped, pushing him out the front door and slamming the screen.

As soon as he left, I continued searching your room, and finally, tucked inside the change purse of your purple Dooney and Bourke bag, I found it: one stick with a blue stripe.

"Damn, Ree Ree!" I slid onto the floor and grabbed my heart as if my hand could hold the pieces together.

So before I got your letter, I discovered why you left. I hadn't a clue before that. Yes, I noticed the weight gain, but I thought you were just getting a little fat. That happens to girls as they get older.

I missed the signs this time. But, Ree Ree, I put you on those pills so this wouldn't happen again! I didn't want you to have to take my walk. It's an uphill haul in the dense forest without a compass! Contrary to what you might think, I wanted better for you. I wanted and still want you to have a better life. What mother doesn't want that for her child? I didn't want you to have to struggle like I do to make ends meet—hoping that after the bills are paid there's a little bit of money left over, creatively stretching a dollar and a meal. Ree Ree, it's hard raising a baby, especially alone—especially at seventeen. I know.

You know I had you when I was fifteen years old. Fifteen! I was still a baby. What the hell did I know about being a mom? Yeah, even back then I had some choices. But I wanted you! I was keeping you. And like you, I blindly thought a baby of my own would just love me. Love me? I thought you would help fill those empty spaces.

Spaces that were created when my daddy walked off and never came back home. When I was ten years old, he left me. He left me with a tired, overworked, resentful, and bitter mother. He left me and he left a hole in my heart. I still needed and wanted him. So, yes, I know what it's like to want someone. I know what it feels like to need someone's love, and know they can't even see you—or feel you. Yes, I know.

Since I couldn't have my daddy anymore, I turned my own womanly body toward those I could easily get, the neighborhood guys.

Roc was who I fell for. Brown skin, tall, good-lookin', dressed in tight Sergio Valente jeans, a nice shirt, and some Stacy Adams, Roc was the one. He was out of high school. He was cool. He was the "man" on the streets. Every girl wanted him. And the boys just wanted to be down with him. When Roc looked my way, talking that mumbled sweet talk, I knew he was the one. I thought getting pregnant with you would seal the deal between me and Roc. I would get an instant family. Love all around. Right?

Well, you see how that turned out. I got duped. Roc was seeing this girl who lived in Yeadon too. The worst part about it? I wasn't the only one carrying his child. Within months of each other, you and Eric were born. Roc wasn't steppin' up to the plate to be a father. He didn't even want you or Eric to call him Daddy. So my dream of the traditional happy family died with his rejection. Another hole in my heart.

However, I still vowed that things would be different with you. No, you wouldn't have the dad-and-mom-together thing, but we would be a family. And that's what I tried to do. Just the two of us. From reading your letter I realize you can't see it. But it's true. I tried.

I was determined to bring you up better than Mom Mom did me. There wasn't going to be any secrets. No need to sneak around. I figured if I was up front with you, you would know more. I was taught just to be seen and not heard—to not ask any questions. And when I did ask, Mom Mom would tell me I'd learn about it when I grew up. She never talked to me about sex. Never! She never even taught me about my period. Her mother never told her, so she grew up not telling me jack shit. So since she wouldn't teach me, I learned on the street.

And Ree Ree, the street is no place to learn. It's not exactly filled with accurate information. That's where rumors and urban myths live. I didn't want you to grow up the way I did. I wanted you to be able to ask or tell me anything.

As I look back, maybe I got too comfortable. Perhaps I shouldn't have been so truthful, or should have kept some of my stuff to myself. Maybe in my need to be different from Mom Mom, I turned out to be just like her in some ways.

Change the names, some of the facts and places, and I could have signed your letter. What you were saying about me is how I feel sometimes about Mom Mom. I didn't know you felt that way about me. It hurts. It hurts my heart, Ree Ree. I thought we were kind of like best friends.

Of course that was the problem, wasn't it? I treated you too much like a friend, instead of a daughter. Even now, at thirty-two, I'm not sure how to be your mother. You and I practically grew up together.

I can remember feeding you a bottle with one hand and doing my GED practice tests with the other. I think I learned about love from you.

So do I know your cry? Hell, yeah! Do you think Mom Mom woke up, changed you, fed you, and burped you in the middle of the night? No, that was me. I was the one who walked to work for three months instead of taking the bus. Do you know why? So I could save money to buy your first bicycle. Now I stand on my feet for eight hours, washing bedpans, changing adult diapers, and cleaning up puke. I do it because it keeps you fed and clothed. If that ain't all love, I don't know what it is.

Can you do that, Ree Ree? Because having a baby is about sacrifice. All those expensive handbags? Practice waving bye-bye. Your child's needs will have to come first. It's gonna be tough. Bye-bye, parties. Bye-bye, freedom. You were searching for love? In a few months, your search will be over. The truth will be if you can stand up to the plate and love someone so much that you're willing to go without so they can have a piece of the world.

Yeah, I have that type of love for you. I'm not the type to walk around saying it all of the time. No, that's not my style. Or hugging and kissing you every minute. I did do that when you were a baby, though!

But getting up, going to work every day, buying you nice clothes—that's my way of showing you love.

Love brought you here; love kept you with me. Mom Mom wanted me to give you to some distant cousin in North Carolina who couldn't have children. We butted heads for a few months over that. The stress at home and stress of the pregnancy combined, eventually made schoolwork difficult. So I dropped out of high school. But it was because of you that I didn't give up. I got my GED. I didn't have to do that. I could have been like some of these people around here and just gone on the system, collected a check each month. But no, I really wanted better for you. I wanted you to see me doing better. And I wanted you to love me for it.

Yeah, sometimes I smoke and hang out at Regal's. That's called tryin' to forget—trying to forget what I could have been or done if I had been smarter, just a little bit smarter. If I had waited until I was educated, married, and older to have you. Done things in the right order. The way I wanted you to do it.

Maybe if I had stayed in school longer I would have been able to help you with your work. But that homework you brought home confused me. I couldn't tell you that, though. How would you ever learn it knowing I gave up? So I just told you, you could t out. What else could I say, Ree Ree?

you know what? I was proud when you got good report card. Really, I was! Do you know where that report card is? You don't have it. Ever since that day you brought it home, I've had it. It's tucked inside your baby album. I bragged to everyone at the nursing home about that report card. Showed it to all of my coworkers and some of the patients, too. Told them all how smart you are. Now I see that I should have told you, too. I guess I didn't because I thought you'd get a big head or something, or maybe think you were smarter than me. And you know, that's funny. Because I really want you to be smarter than me—but not act like you are smarter.

I wanted you to see and do all of the things I missed out on. I didn't just miss out because I had you. But also because I played around in school and was boy crazy. I spent too much time in the streets—running from my mom, chasing after my daddy's love, and ending up with guys like Roc.

I never realized how most of the Rodneys, Nates, etc., are similar to Roc. I figured if I didn't give them my heart and I kept them at a distance, I wouldn't end up hurt. Never once did I think about how their presence might affect you. I was just lookin' for fun, no commitments. Didn't think you needed a daddy. In a

way, if I were to be totally honest, I was also searching for that four-letter word. But I was using the
undercover approach, still protecting my own heart.

Now when I look at you, I mean really look at
you, I see how much you are following me. Despite
my best efforts, it's happening. My efforts to lead you
to something better have you retracing my steps.
Damon? He's a young Roc. I think that's why I liked
him so much. But like Roc was for me, Damon is
much too old for you. I never stopped to see how
Damon can be controlling, too—telling you what to
do, what to wear, meeting only on his terms.
Honestly, Ree Ree, baby, I didn't see that before. But
it's so evident to me now. No, Damon has to go! He
may be twenty-two, but he's not a man. I'm afraid
your friend Austin is right. Damon's not a real man.
Otherwise, he would be taking care of the kids he has.
I don't know what lies he has told you, but experience
shows that he isn't gonna be any different just because
it's your child. What makes me so sure? Because those
other two boys are his too; they're not just their
mama's. And where is he? This baby will be special to
you, but don't expect it to be for him. He's been
there; he's done that. And he hasn't done it well! So,
Ree Ree, where do we go from here?

You're gonna have a baby soon. Do you really

want to have it alone in a homeless shelter? I know, time and time again I told you I'd kick you out if you got pregnant. But I never meant it! That was just me talking tough. You know how we Jemisons do. Rightly or wrongly, you learned that tough talk from me too. My threat was supposed to scare your butt, so you wouldn't let this happen to you. But here you are four months pregnant and I want you home.

Yes. This is a home. Yes. This is *your* home. I know what it's like to raise a baby alone. You are not alone. I am here. I'm always going to be here for you. Roc might not be that bridge (and I'll *deal* with Nettie Johnston), but I am. I'm always gonna be.

And you know what, Ree Ree? There's nothing wrong with wildflowers; they are beautiful. You are beautiful! I happen to love wildflowers too. And there's no one here on this earth that I love more than you. What Mom Mom and even my grandmom forgot to see was the beauty in wildflowers. They truly are a gift to us. As the years passed, I, too, overlooked God's gift. My one chance to grow something on my own and I allowed weeds in my garden. Clipping back. Giving boundaries. Each would have helped your growth. Ree Ree, you don't want to make the same mistakes I did. Come back home. We can be gardeners together, raising your rose. A Black Jade,

160

perhaps? Something that doesn't grow in just any season, but through relentless feeding and pruning? Between the two of us, I'm sure we'll find a way to make her or him bloom.

I miss you and I love you!

Love always,

Mom

PS: Those four words you were waiting for? IT WASN'T YOUR FAULT! Although you unjustly felt the brunt of my anger, it was myself that I was angriest with. Bringing Kevin into our home poisoned it. I couldn't forgive myself for allowing him near you. I'm sorry, Ree Ree. It was never your fault.

GROWING
SEASON

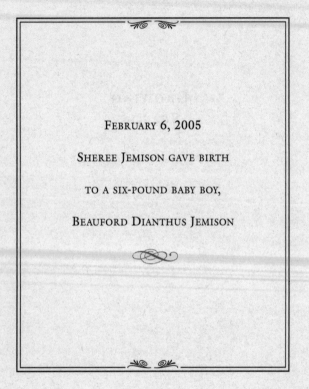

FEBRUARY 6, 2005

SHEREE JEMISON GAVE BIRTH

TO A SIX-POUND BABY BOY,

BEAUFORD DIANTHUS JEMISON

AUGUST 21, 2005

Dear Beauford,

It probably seems strange reading an old letter from me. Countless times I'll tell you the story, but I know if I don't write it down, somehow it'll be forgotten. History has a way of dulling the pain, righting wrongs, and changing facts. I don't want that to happen. What was, is what was. No need to keep secrets or gloss over. The truth is the truth.

It took me a while to accept the truth as it is. In fact it took some special friends, Porsha and Dionny, to bring the mirror to my face. Last August, when I first met the two, I was running away from Moms and my old way of life. I ran to Milagro House, a homeless shelter for young women. I thought since it was a shelter, Milagro House would protect me from my pains, from myself, and from Moms. Instead, the counselors made me bring my wounds to the surface by doing something they called writing therapy. This letter is a part of it, a continuing journal started at Milagro House. It forces me to stop burying the hurts. Instead, I am encouraged to write down all of my pain, see it in print, relive it, and let it go.

While the counselors worked on that type of healing, Porsha and Dionny did their own meddling. The first day I walked into the house with my overpacked suitcase, Porsha and Dionny were all in my business.

"So, I hear you're pregnant," Porsha said while she sat watching TV in the common area.

"You know who the father is?" Dionny asked.

Strangely enough, I found myself nodding and answering their questions. There was something about their tough demeanor that let me know these two girls were no joke. In the beginning, I was a little intimidated by them, so I didn't mouth off. Also, I didn't want to cause any problems and be kicked out. Plus, my reputation hadn't preceded me. Everybody back in Ardmore knew who I was and my reputation for not taking shit, but at the house I was one of seventeen girls with a hard edge. Most of the girls, like Porsha and Dionny, were harder than I was. They had experienced more than I cared to see. So I didn't front. I let them take me under their wing as I listened to their stories.

Porsha was twenty-one and had been at Milagro House for only six months. Before that, she was at a drug treatment center.

"It was get help or go to prison. At first I wasn't ready to stop, but I definitely wasn't ready to do no serious time, either. So I told my lawyer to hook it up," Porsha explained to me one afternoon.

It was Porsha's third time being convicted of snatching pocketbooks. Only, her love wasn't the designer purse, but it's contents. Inside the fancy bags was money, money that would feed Porsha's crack addiction. Being hooked not only caused her to steal, but also to lose her two children.

"Here's a picture of Destiny. She's, like, a year and a half. And this is Kayshawn. He's three," Porsha said as she pointed to her kids' pictures.

The treatment center helped Porsha get clean, but Milagro House was helping Porsha get her life together. Every Wednesday a social worker brought Porsha's two children to the house to visit their mom. Porsha would be so excited waitin' for them to arrive and so sad when her babies left.

Dionny and I would often try to cheer her up or make her laugh, or sometimes we just all sat on the bed and cried together.

Dionny, who was twenty, had been at Milagro

House the longest, thirteen months. She went there because her mom up and moved away, leaving Dionny and her brother unable to pay rent on their apartment.

"Jackie always put dick in front of her kids," Dionny said, talking about her mom.

Dionny and her brother had practically raised themselves while their mother slept all over town. Neither knew their father and they doubted their mom did either. Dionny also wasn't certain who was the father of her own one-year-old daughter, Kimba.

"Kimba kind of looks like this guy from up the street named Romeo. But her head is shaped like some other guy, Abdul, I was messin' with," Dionny said.

When Dionny told her stories, I had to remind myself not judge her, remind myself to look at my own situation. Dionny did exactly what she was taught. However, she will be the first to admit she's changing. Milagro House makes Dionny take parenting classes so she can unlearn many of her mother's mistakes.

Troubling circumstances brought Porsha, Dionny, and many of the other girls to Milagro House. For many, a room in the house literally was the only place keeping them from livin' on the streets.

I thought that's what it was for me too—a bridge. But to hear Porsha and Dionny tell it, I was keeping someone worse off than me from having a room. They thought I was taking up space.

"Yo, Sheree, you need to listen to your mom and go back home," Dionny urged.

Porsha agreed. "Yeah. Why you not givin' her another chance? I wish my mom would write me a letter like that, or call every day begging me to come home."

I tried explaining. "Y'all don't understand what it's like; her boyfriends comin' and goin'; Mom's smokin' all the time."

"So. Leave the room. You say none of the men bother you no more; you sleep with your door locked. Man, that ain't nothin'. Besides, your mom said she wasn't gonna live like that no more," Porsha said.

Dionny added, "Sheree, Milagro House is cool; the counselors here be nice and all, but I always be worryin' 'bout what am I gonna do when it's time for me to leave here. Am I gonna be able to find a place and live on my own? You're lucky; you got a mom who's got your back. You should at least give her one more chance."

I wondered if Moms really had my back this time.

Night after night, Porsha and Dionny pressured me into going back home. As I listened to other girls' stories, I began to think that perhaps I was fortunate.

Although Moms had her faults, she loved me in her own way. She was even willing to change some and help me. If Moms could try to change, maybe I could too.

So on September 24, I agreed to move back home. Porsha and Dionny and the counselors at Milagro House helped awaken me. Once my heart was opened, my head began to see too, and then my growth began. But it was a slow process with little sprouts.

Walking back in through the doors that I had left through more than a month before was weird. The furniture downstairs was still the same, my bedroom untouched. I wondered if the sheets were changed. Everything looked the same, and yet I felt different.

At first Moms and I were tiptoeing around each other, tryin' not to say or do anything to set the other one off. Our dance couldn't last long; eventually the song would end and real talking would happen.

"So, Ree Ree, are you going back to school on Monday?"

I shook my head. "Moms, I think I'm just gonna get my GED. I missed almost a month of school already. Even with the classes I took at Milagro House, I'm probably still behind."

Moms's voice took a more serious turn. "No, Ree Ree,

you misunderstood me. You *are* going to finish school and get your diploma, not your GED. I'll go with you on Monday and talk to the principal, your counselor, whoever I need to talk to, to help you get caught up, 'cause you *are* graduating."

"But, Moms, I don't want to walk around school pregnant."

Moms pulled out a cigarette. "What's the difference between around here and school?" She looked at me and put the smokes away. "You wanted this, right?"

My head dropped into my hands as I nodded and quietly sulked. How could I put into words what I was feelin' when I wasn't sure myself?

School was the last place I wanted to be. Although I was five months pregnant, depending on which clothes I wore, I was barely showing. My breasts and butt seemed to be carrying the brunt of the weight. Not that I needed any more roundness in either spot, but it was better than my stomach. And who knew how long my belly would keep my secret? Damon and Ange already knew. If I went back to school, all of my classmates would soon too. Their snickers wouldn't hurt as much as the reaction I would get from Austin.

At Moms's insistence, I returned to school, so seeing Austin was inevitable. On my first day back, our paths crossed.

Stopping me in the hallway, Austin tapped my shoulder. "Yo, Sheree, where you been?"

Rushing to get to their next class, students bumped and pushed us. Although others surrounded me and Austin, for a minute it felt like it was just me and him in that narrow hallway. It was good to see Austin; of course, he looked good too.

Gently I smiled. Then I remembered the last time I saw Austin Stewart III. My smile was replaced by a feelin' of embarrassment.

"Hey, Austin. How you doin'?" I asked.

"Me? I'm cool, been here. Where have you been? Everybody's been wondering where you were," he said.

"I've been here and there; you know me," I said while cradling my books tightly in front of my stomach.

"You look good." Austin circled me. "Somethin' about you is different, though. I know; you finally left that nut-head Damon alone?"

I wished I could have been honest with myself and honest with Austin and just admitted that Damon skipped out on me, but my pride wouldn't let me form the words and my heart was still hoping that what I eventually did say would come true.

"Me and Damon ain't seein' eye to eye right now. We'll be back together soon."

Reading through my baloney, Austin probed, "Oh,

so he gave you the boot? You don't need him anyway."

Without thinking, I snapped, "Yeah, I do! I'm pregnant!"

I'm sure some other students were still in the hall; the bell may have even rung; but the hallway and Austin were dead silent. As I watched his face, it seemed to be searchin' for an expression, as he was also looking for the right words.

"Sheree . . . I . . . I—"

"Look. Austin, it's okay. I know you didn't know and neither does anybody else here, but some teachers and Ange, so please keep it on the DL."

Austin touched my arm. "You know I don't have oral diarrhea; your secret is safe with me. Look, I'm late and Mrs. Pugh will give me detention if I'm any later. Call me tonight, a'ight?"

Talking over the phone, I wouldn't have to see the disappointment in Austin's face. I still don't know why he cared anyway.

The rest of the day was just like all the others: boring. Ange and I only got to spend a little bit of time together. She was doin' cooperative opportunities (co-op), which means she went to school in the morning for half the day and worked at a hair salon in the afternoons, so we didn't even get to eat lunch together. I was basically on my own.

When I came home, I walked by the courts and saw Damon and his boyees hangin' around. Aside from the changing of the leaves, the court looked no different. Everyone seemed surprised to see me. I'm not sure why Damon was, though; I left umpteen messages on his cell sayin' I was back home.

"Hey, Damon. Can we talk now?" I didn't have the energy or the time to hide my attitude. It had been a long school day.

Damon looked at his boyees for a second. I think he was tryin' to figure out how he could avoid conversatin' with me, because when he looked at me again I could tell he was reading me. Hands on hips, crackin' my gum, for the first time ever, I gave Damon a don't-play-with-me look. Understanding, Damon dismissed his boyees. When they cleared, he nodded.

Like the puppet I was slowly becoming, I spoke, holding the anger so the strings wouldn't break. "I know you got my messages that I'm back home now. How come you never called or visited me?"

Damon looked away. "I've been busy, takin' care of thangs."

Rolling my eyes, I moved around into his view. "Damon, this is *your* baby. Are you gonna be here for me or what?"

Finally he looked at me. "Sheree, I told you I didn't

want no more kids. I'm not tryin' to do this again."

Pleading, I went on. "But it's yours and it's way too late to do anything about it now. On Friday, I'm'a find out if it's a girl. You wanna come with me?"

Seconds. Minutes. Time ticked away as I waited for Damon to answer me. Getting up, he answered, "I'll see what I can do." Then he walked away, leaving me there alone.

Friday afternoon, I looked for Damon at the courts and the corner, checked to see if his car was at his mom's house. I couldn't find him or reach him on his cell. When Moms honked the horn, I ran outside thinking—hoping—it was Damon ready to take me to my appointment. Hiding my disappointment, I slid into Moms's car.

The entire ride I silently hoped that Damon would surprise me and meet me at the doctor's office. However, when Moms and I got there we were the only people in the small lobby. As we were led to the examining room, I kept looking back, waiting, hoping. When we got to the room my mind was still on Damon, but I did as I was told and lifted my shirt and pulled my jeans below my hips and hopped onto the examining table.

"This little thing right here." The ultrasound technician pointed her long, pale, skinny finger at the dark screen. "This is a penis. It's a boy."

"A boy?" Moms sounded excited. "Are you sure? This will be the first boy in our family."

Moving the thingy around on my stomach, the technician showed Moms the penis again. The two of them couldn't stop talking. I needed quiet. Needed time to think. A boy? I wasn't expecting that! I just knew I was havin' a girl. *What am I gonna do with a boy?* I thought.

Since Damon never came to the appointment, I wondered if he somehow knew. Maybe he only makes boys. Damon already had two boys. I was sure having a girl would turn him around, help me to keep him. To be his numero uno like we used to be months ago.

As we were driving home, Moms finally noticed my lack of excitement.

"What's wrong, Ree Ree?"

"Nothing." I sulked.

"C'mon, tell me. What? You mad cause the doctor said you need to gain more weight?"

I shook my head. Moms pulled up in front of the house. Miss Candy was sittin' on the stoop.

"Hey, Mommy." Miss Candy started callin' me that a few days before. I said hi and walked into the house.

I heard her ask what was wrong with me. While I was climbing the stairs to go to bed, Moms was giving what had become her customary answer for all of my moods. "She's pregnant; that's what's wrong."

As I shut the door, I could hear them goin' on about their own young pregnancies.

I didn't hear them leave, but I knew they went to Regal's. Since I'd gotten pregnant, Moms had stopped smokin' cigarettes and weed around me, but she wasn't givin' up Regal's for no one. When I agreed to come back home, she promised that there wouldn't be a lot of different men coming and going. It was just getting dark outside when I woke up at seven thirty. Since I had missed dinner, I was starving. What shocked me was there was actually food in the house. While I was making a steak sandwich, I hit Damon on his cell. For once, he answered.

"Hey. Moms's at Regal's and I'm here by myself. . . . Okay, see you soon."

Waiting for Damon, I talked to Ange on her cell. She was at the high school football game. Ange wanted me to go with her, but I didn't feel like it. I felt myself pulling away from stuff like that. High school seemed so small to me now. Just as I was telling Ange I was havin' a boy, Damon knocked on the door.

Hanging up with her and letting him in, my mind was thinkin' of how to handle this, the best way to break the news to Damon. As I looked at him, I knew he didn't want to talk. His mannerisms, his eyes, told me the deal, so I did what I always do when I want Damon's attention. I gave him some. I put it on him and hoped that would remind him of how good it used to be.

Damon stayed for a bit, but he never asked about my appointment. He didn't even offer an excuse as to why he didn't come. Disappointed, I couldn't bring myself to tell him the news. After receiving a call and talkin' to some girl, he bounced. In the past, Damon would have acted like the chick was one of his boyees. Now he openly talked, made dates, and sounded all too happy to hear their voices. Evil thoughts crept inside my head, wishing him and her harm. I don't know why I asked him to come.

In October, the secret was out! There was no more hiding anything with large shirts and sweats. My belly button even popped! At first, people at school, those that knew me, were a little distant. I think they thought I was contagious or somethin'. Some of their reactions hurt a bit, causing me to be somewhat embarrassed by my situation. Eventually, as high schoolers often do, they moved on to somethin' else. I was no longer the hot topic and folks started actin' normal again. Every once and again, I'd catch somebody whisperin', though.

Some of my teachers were probably the worst. Even though I couldn't hear what they were sayin', I could tell they were often talking about me. Oftentimes I would hang my head and try not to be seen. My stomach definitely told the world my business. I had had unprotected sex, something our health and gym teachers had definitely warned against.

My predicament must have told the teachers I had never listened at all. If they didn't give me such judging looks, I would have told them I planned this. This was no accident. Not really. My history teacher shook his head every time I walked into class. You'd think he'd have gotten used to seein' me and my belly. My math teacher often broke her face up looking as though she felt sorry for me or somethin'. My guidance counselor didn't look at me differently, but he made it a point to stay on my case. He kept buggin' me, wanting to know what I was gonna do afterward.

All of it was enough to make me want to quit! I was tired; my feet were beginning to swell; my thighs started rubbin' together. I had to pee all the time and school just was a difficult place to be. But Moms wasn't hearin' me. She wouldn't allow me to drop out. I even tried to get Porsha and Dionny to help me persuade Mom. But they were no help. Porsha and Dionny said quitting was stupid. They reminded me of Porsha's struggle. She had taken the GED test three times and still hadn't passed.

Porsha told me on the phone one night, "Girl, the GED is hard. Every time I sit there takin' that test, I beat myself up for havin' dropped out of school. I only had a semester left and I would have had my diploma, but no, I wanted to hang out, so I quit. That was one of the stupidest things I ever did. You try remembering all of the math formulas and grammar rules and stuff. It's easier stayin' in school and doin' it that way."

So between Moms and Porsha and Dionny, my butt stayed in school. I was certain Ange and Austin would have basically said the same thing in their own way, so I didn't even unveil my plans. The last thing I felt like hearing was another lecture. My ears took quite the beatin' from a surprise visit from Roc one afternoon in the living room.

"Sheree, your mom told me about your situation."

Situation? I laughed to myself. He couldn't even say it—say that I was gonna have a baby.

"I don't know why you got yourself into this. How are you going to raise a baby when you're still young yourself? This is going to be your responsibility, not mine and not your mom's. You hear?" Roc asked.

Yes. Roc, the man who gave me life but nothin' more, was tryin' to talk to me about responsibility. Normally, I would have held my tongue, acted like I was listenin', cracked my gum, rolled my eyes, and walked away. But the last few months of my pregnancy, I lost my ability to think before speaking. Whatever was on my mind flew out of my mouth—unedited.

"Look, Roc, don't try to play daddy now. It's seventeen years and five months too late. When I needed you to be one, you weren't here. Did you ever think that maybe I wouldn't be in this, in this . . . SITUATION if you had been a real dad?" Rolling my eyes, I stomped up the stairs to the bathroom to pee.

Apparently shocked by my behavior, Roc was talkin' to Moms.

"She's just like you, Stacey! Evil! You were so evil when you were pregnant. I want my little girl back," Roc said.

Moms's cool reply let me know she was enjoying this. "Yeah, well she wasn't lying, now was she?" I heard Roc walking around. Moms must have lit a cigarette, 'cause her voice sounded full of air. "But you're here now and Sheree will come around; it may just take her a while. In the past, she hasn't been able to count on you."

Roc actually sounded sad. "Yeah. I know. I'm doin' my best."

Holding nothing back, Moms replied, "Roc, you've got to come better than your best. I've seen what you think is your best and it ain't shit. Ree Ree really needs you right now."

Expecting their conversation to take a turn for the worse, I pressed my ear to the bathroom door. Surprisingly, Roc didn't get defensive. He seemed to be listening to Moms.

"So, did you talk to Nettie?" Moms asked.

Talk to Nettie about what, I wondered.

"Yeah," Roc said.

Pressing my ear, I strained to hear their low voices. I think I liked it better when they yelled.

"Well, as long as you set her straight, I'll be cool. But I'm'a tell you, just like I told her, if she messes with mine, I'm comin' after her. That means no snide comments, no interfering between you and Ree Ree, and no making her wait in the hall." Moms laid it out.

"Stacey, it's cool," Roc said in his cool voice.

"Whatchu see in her anyway?" Moms laughed. "She's not even a little bit pretty."

I banged my forehead on the door laughin' at that

one. So they wouldn't know I was dippin', I went into my bedroom, shut the door, and sat on the floor by the heating vent.

I missed Roc's response, if he did answer. They were both laughin' about somethin'. Roc's voice broke through the laughter.

"Well, I better get going," he said.

"You don't have to leave so soon. Ree Ree probably laid down. She's getting near her last trimester, and she gets tired more. She'll be up again soon."

"Nah, I'd better get going. Gotta see Lil' Roc before he goes to bed."

The front door opened and closed. I was sure Roc had left, so I got into bed, closed my eyes, and prayed to God. Not being religious, I'm never sure if I'm doin' it right, because my prayers never seem to be answered. But I begged God to change Damon. If Roc can sit up here and talk to Moms like that, surely Damon can come around.

Four weeks later, I was in my seventh month, still reciting the same prayer and now hoping for what looked like it would be a miracle. Damon hadn't been to any of my doctor's appointments. Sometimes he'd made promises.

"Okay, tomorrow at four. . . . Yeah, I got the address," Damon would say.

But he'd never show up. I'd hit his cell at 4:05 and get his voice mail: "Damon, where are you? It's after four. I'm at my doctor's appointment. They're runnin' behind, so you still have time to get here. I probably won't see the doctor until four thirty."

While waiting to see the doctor, I'd keep my eyes glued to the waiting room door. Don't ask me why. I was seven months pregnant and he hadn't been to one appointment. Why would he start then? But still I hoped and prayed. By four forty-five, I was leaving the doctor's office holding another empty urine cup. Fuming, I'd light up Damon's cell.

"Why do you always pull this shit? Why can't you grow up? Be a man! And take care of your responsibilities? I hate you sometimes!" I'd slam down my phone.

Walking home from the doctor's office, I'd eventually cool down. By the time I walked through the door I would feel bad for being like that. I'd call apologizing, making my own excuses.

"Look, Damon, I'm sorry for quirkin' out like that. You make me so mad sometimes. You say you're comin' to the doctor's with me and then you're a no-show. What am I supposed to think? I know you're busy, but, Boo, I need you right now. This baby, our baby, needs you. So I'm sorry—a'ight? Call me; I'll be here."

Damon rarely called. I was doin' all of the callin', talkin' to his voice mail more than to him. The few times we did talk, Damon never asked about my appointments or any other details. His indifference infuriated and hurt me. I often locked myself in my bedroom, hoping sleep would lessen the pain.

But as my belly continued to stretch, sleep was becoming harder and harder. If you weren't kickin' my ribs, then you were sitting on my bladder, forcing me to get up every few hours to pee less than a shot glass full of urine. Either due to lack of sleep or Damon's trippin', my moods were all over the place.

I was grumpy in school.

"You're huge!" Austin said to me one day in the hallway.

My butt was so big it looked like *it* was havin' the baby. I knew what I looked like, checked in the mirror every morning and night for signs of a stretch mark. What I didn't need was everyone reminding me how big I was getting.

Swiveling my eyes and neck, I said, "Go to hell, Austin." Then I waddled to my next class.

Another day, Ange brought me to tears as she gave me a thick piece of tiramisu from her aunt and uncle's sandwich shop.

"Here." Ange handed me a card. "Aunt Carlita and Uncle Louie told me to give this to you too."

It was a fifty-dollar gift card to a baby store.

"Thank you. They didn't have to—"

Ange stopped me. "They wanted to. You're like family; you know they love you. And Daddy and Mom want to know what you need—a crib, a stroller?"

As I gave Ange a confused look, she explained. "Yes, Daddy wanted to know what you needed. He asked me. We talked about his comments and I finally told Daddy off. I told him how wrong he is for treating you the way he does. I told him how you're the only one of my friends who actually tries to help me, keep me out of trouble. And you know what? Daddy actually said he was sorry. I'm beginning to think I should have talked to him about a lot of things a long time ago."

It was no secret that Mr. Rinaldi hadn't particularly liked me. He was critical about me being pregnant, going so far as to order Ange to find another friend and to keep away from me. I knew our friendship ran too deep for her to just drop me. I figured she would do like she usually did when he forbid somethin': sneak behind Mr. Rinaldi's back. But for once, Ange stood up for herself, tellin' him no and explaining why. I'm convinced Mr. Rinaldi changed his view because Ange was finally straight up. Either way, it was great to hear that my best friend's father finally approved of our friendship. That news caused my eyes to betray me. I couldn't hold back the tears, which kept runnin' down my face. Having never seen me cry before, not even happy tears, Ange was shocked by my reaction. I was becoming used to the sudden waterfall. Lately it seemed that crying and moping were all I did.

However, usually my tears were reserved for my bedroom, where they were supposed to be between God and me. But Moms wasn't fooled, so one night she came into my room, offering me tissues and some advice.

"Ree Ree, you've got to let him go. This isn't good for the baby. It's not good to be sad all the time. I know it hurts. I know Damon is hurting you, but you've gotta think of the baby."

I blurted, "I am thinkin' of the baby. What am I gonna tell him? Your dad didn't want you?" I screamed.

Walking over, Moms put her arm around me. Softly she said, "Whatever the truth is, you'll tell him that."

I looked at Moms, and the hold on my tear ducts loosened. She made it sound so simple. But as I recall, that's how she explained Roc to me.

I was a little girl. I think I was in the first grade. Everyone had to stand up and say somethin' about the members of their family. Of course, not everyone had the traditional family unit, but no one called their dad by his first name, either. Everybody laughed at me when I said Roc and not Daddy. At first I thought they were thinkin' Rock, and yeah, having a dad named Rock, like a stone, was funny. So I quickly corrected the class and spelled Roc's name. Then Susan O'Hara raised her hand, red curls bouncing about, and asked, "Why do you call your dad Roc? That's weird."

Confused, I answered, "Because that's what I'm supposed to call him. Everybody calls him that. My half brother Eric calls him that too."

The teacher, Mrs. Rabinowitz, attempted to smooth things over. "Roc isn't her real daddy; he's her play daddy. Okay, Andrew, it's your turn. Thank you, Sheree."

"B-but . . . ," I stuttered.

Hushing me, Mrs. Rabinowitz said, "Thank you. That will be all, Sheree."

As soon as Moms picked me up from the babysitter, I lit into her, wanting to know why she never told me Roc wasn't my dad.

"What!" Moms yelled. "Where the hell did you get that?"

Through tears, I recounted the classroom activity, my schoolmates' laughter, their comments, and the teacher's. Every remark was repeated.

"Ree Ree, Roc is your dad. Don't ever let anyone tell you differently. He's your father. Even though you don't call him Dad, that doesn't make it any less true."

I questioned, "How come I can't call him Daddy, then?"

Even at that young age, I could see Moms's wheels turning, tryin' to figure out how to answer me. Thinkin' it through, she finally answered.

"Roc is part of an old-school way of thinking that thinks it's cool to have their kids call them by their first name. Since he doesn't come around much or pay much support, I don't think he deserves the title of Daddy—no way. But mark my words, Ree Ree, one day Roc is gonna wish you called him that. One day he'll learn what it takes to be one and see how special that honor, that word, really is."

It had taken seventeen years, but maybe Moms's message was coming true. Roc was coming around the house more. At first, he seemed to be so disappointed in me. That was new to me, considering he never acted like he cared before. As my due date drew nearer, though, Roc's disappointment seemed to fade. He finally started referring to my "situation" as the baby. He seemed to be getting excited, too.

On Thanksgiving Day, Roc and Lil' Roc stopped by Mom Mom's. That's where Moms, Rodney, and I had dinner. I called and left, like, four messages on Damon's cell phone, inviting him to join us too, but like usual, he never called me back. So I spent the day grumpy. When Roc and Lil' Roc came by, that surprise brightened up my mood a bit.

"Sheree, can I feel the baby kick?" Lil' Roc asked.

I jiggled my stomach trying to get some movement. He placed his little hand on what I thought was an enormous belly, but the doctor still insisted wasn't big enough. "Here, right here. Did you feel that? That was the baby," I told him.

"Is it a boy or a girl?" he asked.

I sighed. "It's a boy; his name is Damon."

Ever inquisitive, Lil' Roc asked, "Damon? Who's that? Aren't you going to name him Roc?"

Roc stepped in, patting Lil' Roc. "Yeah, Roc would be nice, huh?"

"There's already enough Rocs around here," I said, my sour mood returning.

But Moms jumped in. "And enough Damons! Give my grandbaby a fresh start."

"Moms, don't start. His name will be Damon the Second."

"I know one thing; I'm not calling him Damon," Roc stated.

Determined to stick with his dad, Lil' Roc echoed, "Me neither, Daddy."

We all fell out laughin'. Fortunately, somebody changed the subject and started talking about Mom Mom's amaryllises. She was trying to get them to bloom in time for Christmas. As the others talked, I was able to slip back into the corners of my mind. I wasn't sure what to do about Damon. I thought he'd come around by now. The last time I'd seen him, I mean really seen him, was in October. We had never been apart that long. I thought for sure he'd be back, at least . . . but he didn't even want that no more. An old friend named Tammy happily informed me that Damon was seein' some girl named Keisha. It wasn't news that I wanted to hear. I wanted to know how I could get Damon to stop iggin' me.

"Here." Mom Mom's easy voice brought me out of

my dark hole and back into the room. "Here's your plate, baby."

Grabbing it, I thanked her and looked at all of the vegetables she had piled on there.

"Mom Mom, you know I don't like collard greens or green beans," I said, pouting.

Between the green vegetables were some sweet potatoes, but there was barely room for turkey or stuffing.

"Baby, you've got to eat vegetables; they're good for the baby," Mom Mom scolded.

"I keep tellin' her that, but she doesn't listen to me. The doctor keeps telling her she needs to gain more weight. She's only gained twelve pounds so far. And if she would stop eating potato chips, cheese twists, sodas, cheese steaks, lemon heads, and all that other junk, she would gain more weight."

I felt fat! To me, twelve pounds was too much weight on my curvy body, so I wasn't tryin' to gain any more. Besides, Damon would never want me if I got real big. I couldn't explain this to Mom Mom or anyone else, so with everyone watching me I had no choice but to take a few bites of the veggies. In a way, all of the attention was nice—Mom Mom cut me a big slice of her sweet potato pie—but I'm also not used to all eyes being on me—at least not in that way or by any of them. Before I got pregnant, I got lots of looks and whistles from guys. However, when my belly popped, all of that stopped. Nobody—no guys, cute or ugly—gave me the eye no more.

After Thanksgiving, the madness began. While everyone was counting down the days until Christmas, I was counting down to my due date, February 1, even though Moms and Miss Candy insisted I erase that date from my head. They said babies were like men; they never came on time.

Secretly, I continued to block off the days. It gave me somethin' to do—somethin' other than thinking and worryin' about Damon. That was already takin' up too much of my time, but I couldn't help myself. I wanted him to be there with me, rubbing my swollen feet, feeling the movements in my stomach, or just sitting beside me, chillin'.

A few days before Christmas, Ange asked me to go to King of Prussia Mall with her. She was done with her list and wanted to get some things for herself. Reluctantly, I agreed to go with her. I couldn't stay in my cocoon the whole Christmas holiday. On the way there, Ange chatted about some new guy, Mario, that she was seein'. Even though Ange was my girl, a part of me was a teeny bit jealous. Ange had someone. Mario was a senior at Cardinal Dougherty in Philly. He was half-Italian and full Catholic. Mr. Rinaldi even liked him. At that moment I wanted you to hurry up and arrive so I'd have somebody too.

We shopped around the mall, Ange buying several outfits. My feet, my legs, everything, was getting tired, so we sat down on one of the benches. While we were sitting there, gossiping, I thought my eyes were playin' tricks on me. From a distance, I could see what looked like a fine dark-skinned guy in a soft black leather coat, with a baby blue turtleneck sweater peeking through and matching baby blue Tims. Realizing it was Damon, my Chocolate Thunder, I smiled. Ear to ear. Of all places, I never thought I'd bump into him there. I wondered where his boyees were. I didn't see Bird or Chris; Damon never goes anywhere by himself. I was thinking that maybe he'd called home and Moms told him I was there and he was lookin' for me. Ange was still talkin', but I had no idea about what, when I stood up, still smiling from ear to ear. Damon didn't see me; he was closer, but still a good distance away.

Raising my arm, I was just about to wave and get his attention when he stopped and turned around. Someone was walking up to him but his body was blockin' my view. All I could see, barely see at that, were jeans and another set of matching light blue Tims. I searched my mind. *Does Bird or Chris have blue Tims?* Then I thought about it; Damon and his boyees would never go the twins route. I kept waiting to see who he was with.

Finally, as Damon stepped aside, she moved into view. Even with all the shoppers walking in front of and around them, my eyes were certain she was this girl named Ushama. Damon's whatever-you-want-to-call-her—trick, skeezer, shorty—from the summer. She was also the last person I wanted to see, especially not when I was eight months pregnant.

Tapping Ange's arm, I motioned for her to look ahead. Quickly she spotted Damon. He finally noticed us, too. Making eye contact, I saw Damon look me over—well, stare at my round belly. He whispered somethin' to Ushama and she finally saw me too. With a big smirk on her big-lipped face, Ushama boldly walked right over to me.

I whispered to Ange, "Here we go again. I knew she'd try to start some shit knowin' I'm too big to be fightin'."

Laughing, Ushama taunted, "Ain't you ever heard of the pill or rubbers?"

Crackin' my Big Red, I stepped in her face, laughed, and challenged her. "Damon knew I wasn't a hooker like

195

you, lettin' any-old-body in, so he could ride me bare-back."

Getting defensive and sounding unsure, "That ain't Damon's! Is it, Boo?"

"Oh, so you're her Boo too?" I snapped, staring at Damon. "Damon, you didn't tell this tramp that you're gonna be a daddy again?" I turned back toward Ushama. "That I'll always have a piece of you? That I'm your number one?" I moved within inches of Damon's face, smelling his sweet breath. "Tell her, Damon. Tell her ev-er-y-thing that you whisper in my ear late at night."

Sounding confused, Ushama tried again. "Sheree, ain't nobody listenin' to you and your lies. You should be tryin' to find a daddy for your baby instead of pinning it on Damon. Or, if you're not sure who the daddy is, you know Ricki Lake and Maury can help girls like you out!"

Finally, Damon spoke, "C'mon, Ushama." She stood there lookin' at me. In that quick moment, I made a decision—the decision I should have made several months before when Ushama and I bumped heads.

"You know what, Ushama? This isn't about you, and I ain't got no beef with you. My problem is with Damon. Yes, this is his baby. No need to go

Hollywood; we can keep it local, call one of the radio stations and take the DNA/who's-your-daddy test. Damon was the only person I was with like that for more than a year. So you do the math. It's his and he knows it." Turning to Damon, I sincerely asked, "Why are you doin' me like this?"

With no hint of joking, Damon stated, "Sheree, I don't really know if that's mine. I don't know what you do when I'm not around." Tugging Ushama, he said, "C'mon, Ushama. Bye, Angela."

It's funny, Ushama didn't move right away. I felt her staring at me as my jaw dropped open in disbelief. Shaking my head, I sat back down on the bench and watched Damon and Ushama walk away. Hatred was what I immediately felt for him. Ushama? Our eyes briefly met and I could see that she no longer detested me, but pitied me. I didn't want her pity, but at least she believed me.

As Damon and Ushama walked away, Ange started talkin'. My mind was tired of words, body tired of shoppin'. I just needed to get home, back home and into my bed.

After I had slept away the rest of the day and most of the evening, Moms came into my room.

"Ree Ree, you've got to stop moping around like

197

this. You've got to let Damon go. He's not gonna change. You and this baby aren't gonna make him. I've been through it. Take it from me, the sooner you stop thinkin' about him, the better you'll start feelin'."

I couldn't bring myself to tell her what had happened at the mall. Somehow, I knew she'd understand, but her take on it would be to bad-mouth Damon. I didn't need any more salt on my wound. I had enough unkind words and thoughts regarding him; I didn't need any more. So when Moms left my room, I called Austin.

"Hey, Sheree. What's poppin? Or is that a bad question to ask someone about to have a baby?"

Austin and I talked about the baby, school, and the holidays. Then I told him why I really called.

"I don't know what to tell you. I don't know Damon. It seems to me like your mom is right; maybe you should just forget about him. There's nothing you can do to change him; but you can change yourself, Sheree."

Last summer, Austin was full of unwanted advice; now when I needed his thoughts, I sensed hesitation. He was holding something back.

"Austin, be real, give it to me straight," I urged.

He paused for a few, then spoke. "Look, ask yourself if Damon is really the type of . . . type of . . . I hate to say it, but the type of man you really want around your baby. Yes, he's the father, but he's a drug dealer.

Do you want your son to grow up to be a drug dealer? To look up to his dad that way? You don't have to answer me; just think about it, okay?"

I agreed. Although my brain was getting tired of thinking, it seemed to be all I was doin'. What I really wanted was some easy answer, a magical solution to turn this situation around. Maybe if I thought some more, a bit more, somethin' would come to me.

DECEMBER 25, 2004

Christmas Day. Christmas has always been my favorite holiday. On this Christmas, Santa gave me a taste of what is to come, my Christmas future.

Past Christmases, there were usually boxes of wrapped clothes, CDs, jewelry, and my favorite, some type of pocketbook. This Christmas, a bassinet, infant seat, high chair, and baby bathtub were tucked under the tree. None of the wrapped presents were just for me. They were all somethin' I would need and would use in about one month. When Mom Mom arrived for Christmas dinner carrying several packages, I got excited; surely one of them was for me. As I opened each box, I had to hide my disappointment. Each contained a baby outfit. Cute blue jumper; Moms called it a onesie. A tiny dark blue snowsuit with white snowflakes. A red knit sweater and matching hat. Black sweats with the Sixers logo. All of the outfits were adorable, but none was my size. Politely, I thanked Mom Mom and did my best to keep my lips poked in.

After dinner, Roc arrived carrying a big box. Right away, I knew that one wasn't for me either. Everything I wanted came in small packages. Beaming from ear to ear, Roc watched carefully as I opened his present. It was a stroller.

Roc stood up and pointed to the box. "This isn't just any stroller either. The lady at the store showed me how easy it is to fold and open. You can do it with one hand while holding the baby in the other. It'll be easy for you to collapse and fold as you get on the bus," he explained.

In horror, I asked, "On the bus?"

All eyes were on me. Roc answered, "Yeah, bus, train, trolley, whatever."

Moms interjected. "No, Roc, you missed her point. Ree Ree here thinks she's too good to ride the bus. Thinks she should have a car like her rich friend Angela. Am I right?"

Embarrassed, I hung my head, not sayin' anything. I knew Moms couldn't afford to buy me a car, not even a used one, but still a large part of me wished that she had, could, and would.

Getting a car was a fantasy. But lately I seemed to be living in la-la land. It was much easier to stay in make-believe than to face my reality—that I was too young to have you. I didn't have any money or a job to get some.

Moms continued, "I keep telling you, Ree Ree, once you have a baby, it ain't about you anymore. I had to take the bus, for—what was it, Moms, five years?" Mom Mom nodded. "Yeah, for five years before I had enough money to buy my first car. It was a Hyundai—a used Hyundai at that." Moms laughed.

Then Mom Mom picked up the story. "Yeah, you loved that little car. I remember it had a radio that you could take out, some type of antitheft device. Each night you'd come into the house carrying Sheree in one arm and that radio in the other. I would laugh to myself because nobody in his or her right mind would steal a Hyundai's car radio. But it was yours; you bought it and were determined to take care of it."

"She wouldn't let nobody else drive it either. My car was in the shop once and I asked Stacey if I could borrow it and she wouldn't let me," Roc teased.

Moms laughed. "Oh, no. I worked too hard, skimping and scratching, saving all that money to buy it. What if you had crashed? I'd be back on the bus. Uh-uh. I'd seen what had happened to Candy. She lent

Jamil her car. He was sellin' out of it and the cops took it. It didn't matter that it wasn't his car, that she didn't sell; cops impounded that bad boy and insurance wouldn't cover it. So Candy had to start saving all over again. Nah, nobody but me was driving my car. I was strugglin' enough raising Ree Ree. I didn't need any more setbacks."

"Moms, how am I gonna get a car?" I whined.

Answering as one, they all said, "Get a job!"

Moms added, "*After* you graduate."

Moms made it clear that she had me covered up until then. All I had to do was go to school. But I know it wasn't easy for her. I saw the doctors' bills; those greedy mugs made you pay up front before insurance kicked in at the delivery. And even with health insurance, Moms was coughin' up a lot of dough. She often worked doubles and sometimes filled in on the dreaded overnight weekend shift, all to "get ahead," as she called it. What's amazing is, Moms never complained. She just did it. She probably didn't know it, but it was like I was a little girl again because I found myself watchin' her—watchin' how she got up, made her coffee, showered, put her uniform on, and went to work. She didn't exactly leave with a smile on her face, but she wasn't frownin' or grumbling about it either. And when she came home, sometimes sixteen or seventeen hours later, still no broad smile, but a slight grin. The shift was over; she was home; what was there to grumble about?

Silently, I watched Moms do this, day in and day out. It's funny how time has a way of erasing things, little things, and allowing other memories to creep in and take up space. Somewhere along the way, I forgot that this wasn't new to Moms. As I watched her go to work each day, my mind rolled back, remembering when I was a little girl.

It was before my fifth birthday. My best friend Tammy had her party at Chuck E. Cheese and I wanted to have one there also. But one-stop partying, with food, games, cake, and fun, wasn't cheap. I overheard Moms tellin' Mom Mom that one night after dinner. Within those next few months, Moms was working more, takin' other people's shifts at the pancake house where she worked then. Every night she'd come home looking tired and worn. She'd dump her tip money on the bed, light a cigarette, and begin counting. When she was done, she'd write down the amount on a piece of paper and dump the money into a large cookie tin.

Moms's birthday is exactly two weeks before mine. We'd usually go to Bella Italia for dinner to celebrate. Then later, she'd wear a new outfit that she had just bought herself and go to Regal's with Miss Candy. That year, it wasn't to be. Two weeks before my fifth birthday, on Moms's birthday, she worked overtime. Mom Mom told her we'd go out the next night, but Moms said no, she wasn't doin' all that this year. So we didn't go out and Moms didn't even buy herself anything new. What she did do, though, was take me and four of my friends to Chuck E. Cheese for my birthday. And she gave me a new Barbie and a Barbie Jeep! That goes down as one of my all-time favorite birthdays.

After stepping back in time and then slipping back to the present, I began to feel guilty for being so selfish. Here Moms had worked her butt off tryin' to make me happy, was once again workin' crazy hours so *my* baby could have the best, and I was silently fretting because I didn't get any Christmas presents and wanted my own car.

Yeah, I had a nerve!

But I got myself together and jumped into the Christmas spirit. Miss Candy and Mr. Todd stopped by. Later, Rodney came with Moms's present. It was a gift basket from some bath store. I couldn't tell if Moms was happier with the gift or just the fact that he brought her somethin'. Either way, Moms seemed truly happy as they all danced in the front room. Sitting in the chair, I watched Roc lookin' at Moms and Rodney. I think I saw in his eyes a flash of that green-eyed monster that people are always talkin' about.

He stood up. "Hey, Sheree, Stacey, Miss Kate, I'd better get back. I promised Lil' Roc I'd put his race-track together when I got home," Roc explained.

Moms stopped dancing, grabbed Roc's hand, and said, "Oh, no. One dance and then you can leave."

Trying to act like he didn't want to while movin' to the music, Roc held Moms's hand and they bopped. Who'd have thought that two people who were often at odds could dance so beautifully together? Movin' so gracefully, they looked as though the dance was theirs only. If Rodney noticed any of this, he was playin' it cool. He went into the kitchen and fixed himself another drink. Meanwhile, the DJ on WDAS took us— well, took them, Miss Candy, Moms, Roc, Mr. Todd, and Mr. Rodney—back to 1980.

"Aw, that's it right there! Um, y'all remember?" Miss Candy yelled.

"Remember? Tell her, Roc. This cut used to be our song!" Moms boasted. Roc pulled her tight and they slow danced to Teena Marie's "Young Love."

This was all new to me. I didn't remember ever seein' Moms and Roc behave this way. I knew they both loved to dance, but not together. And a slow song? I knew Moms and Roc's love, like Teena Marie's, had simply grown old, but was it reblossoming?

Before the music changed, so did Moms's partner. Perhaps Rodney was a bit uncomfortable with Roc holdin' Moms like that, 'cause he cut in a few seconds before the last note.

Walking over to me, Roc was grinning. "All right. I think that's my cue to leave." He kissed my cheek. "Merry Christmas, Sheree. I'll see you later."

Normally, I would have taken that as my cue to make a quick exit to my bedroom, but I didn't feel like going up yet. All I would have done was lay in bed, listen to some music, and think about Damon, wonder why he didn't call, stop by, or buy me anything for Christmas. No, I wasn't gonna do that tonight. For one night, I was allowing my thoughts to take a holiday. So instead, I sat with Mom Mom and watched Moms, Miss Candy, and them dance and have fun.

Soon 2005 rolled in, and I was back at school, countin' down the days until February 1. That was my due date and I was determined to be on time. I wanted to hurry up, drop the load, and then get back in shape for track season. I promised my coaches and myself that I was running my final year. They seemed to be doubtful about the possibilities of my running track again. A couple of months before, I'd been certain. "If Marion Jones can come back, so can I," I told the coaches. But as I looked at my fat belly hangin' low on my body, watermelon breasts, and pumpkin butt, secretly I was a little skeptical too. I wondered if I was ever gonna look the same.

February 1 came and went. I stayed home from school that day because I didn't want to go into labor or deliver there. All day, I sat around, one hand on the cordless phone, the other on my belly, waiting. Nothin' happened, not even those false labor pains that the doctors call Braxton Hicks. "Disappointed" isn't a strong enough word to describe how I felt when the day changed to February 2 and I still had a baby inside of me.

I tried to stay home another day, but Moms wasn't havin' that.

"Ree Ree, you don't want to get behind. You'll be missing enough time once the baby comes," she said.

Moms was no joke with this schoolin' stuff. So I went, tried to concentrate, but everybody was askin' about the baby—teachers and classmates. They knew I was due, and since I missed school they assumed . . . but there I was, still fat and still wobblin' to class.

I wished Damon would have taken the same interest. Here I was about to deliver his baby at any minute and he still wasn't visiting or callin'. Mostly he screened my calls, forcing me to leave messages on his voice mail.

"Damon, it's Sheree. Remember me? You're numero uno." I laughed sarcastically. "The one who is pregnant with *your* baby. I haven't heard from you. What's up? I'd like to see you; we *need* to talk. Holla back."

My messages often began with me gettin' with him, but ended with me begging. Neither my calls nor begging prompted Damon to ever call me back. He didn't care about me anymore. I wondered if he ever did.

Between Damon's ignoring me and my lateness, I was one moody mama! Everything—the weather, Ange, school—was getting under my skin and prickling me. Moms just shrugged it off, mumbling something to herself. One evening, after she found me on my hands and knees dusting the baseboards in my bedroom, I overheard her mumblings.

"The baby will be here soon," she said.

"Soon? When?" I asked, but Moms didn't have a definite answer.

The next morning, I woke up feelin' like I had to throw up. Moms kept tryin' to get me to eat something, but my stomach didn't seem to want to accept any visitors, not even toast or tea. I was sure if I ate, I'd bring it back up. Topping off the nausea, I had a raw deal on both ends! Even though I wasn't eating anything, somethin' was running through me. I had diarrhea. Sure that I had food poisoning, I told Moms to call the doctor. Instead, she laughed.

"Ree Ree, you're probably in early labor. The baby will be here soon. Why don't you try to get some rest?" Moms suggested.

Rest? With a baby about to come? No way, I wanted to get this thing over with. If the baby was comin', I wanted to be awake, fully alert. I actually thought I could sleep through labor. Besides, even if I wanted to, I couldn't sleep. My mind was racing, a million thoughts sprinting through my head. I kept wondering if I should call Damon; if it was gonna hurt; if Damon would see you being born; if I could change my mind about the whole thing. While my brain conjured up unanswered questions, my lower back slowly began to throb.

Throughout the morning and into the afternoon, the pain in my back got worse. Moms tried to make the pain go away by putting a heating pad on it, but that only helped a little bit. I was lying on the couch watching *106 & Park* when I got a sharp pain in my stomach. It felt like I had cramps. Fortunately, the pain would come and go.

"He'll be here soon, Ree Ree," Moms said when I described the pains.

I was sick of her responses. Soon wasn't soon enough. She hadn't started timing the pains or said we should go to Bryn Mawr Hospital, so we waited. Moms passed the time reminiscing about my birthday.

"Did I ever tell you I was walking home from the Pike when my water broke?" I nodded my head. She continued anyway. "Yep, I walked to the five-and-ten to get a perm. I needed a touch-up in the worst way. Candy promised to give me one that night. All day I had some pains in my stomach, but I thought it was gas, not contractions. It didn't really hurt that bad. Everybody had been telling me labor hurt. So I walked myself up to the Pike, bought my Dark and Lovely, and was walking back, when *bam*, my water broke. I was right near Mrs. Simpkins' house when it happened. Sopping wet, I knocked on her door and she made Mr. Simpkins drive me home. Mr. Simpkins thinks he had a hand in helping to deliver you. Even now, he teases me and says you were almost born in his car. Of course he's exaggerating a bit, but I suppose he thought that by the way I was screaming in his car. Because once my water broke, the real pain began. Those ladies weren't lyin' about labor pains."

On one level, I understood Moms was tryin' to comfort me—make me feel better, any way she could.

But my pains were getting faster and stronger. I was scared. Talking and listening were beginning to aggravate me. When I stood up to walk to the bathroom, a flood of water soaked my panties and sweatpants. Thinking I had held it too long and finally peed my pants, my eyes teared up in frustration. My body was no longer under my control. I was powerless against a little baby. Sitting in the chair, watchin' me, Moms busted out laughin'. My piercing glare let her know that I failed to see the humor.

"Ooh, your water done broke. It's time to go to the hospital. I'll call Candy and Roc."

My water? I was relieved that I hadn't peed myself!

As Moms made the calls and grabbed the bag, I changed into another pair of sweats and undies. She should have told me changing was useless. I discovered that the water doesn't just break and that's it. No, I trickled and gushed water all the way to the emergency room. Miss Candy rode with us to the hospital, her and Moms gabbin' about God knows what the whole way. It seemed like Moms was takin' the long route and purposely hitting every pothole, speed bump, and manhole on the road. Each bump and sudden start or stop made my area down there hurt.

By then, the pain was moving from my back around to my front, and back again to my butt. With each contraction, it felt like you were gonna fall out of my butt and onto the floor.

After I was put in a room and in a hospital gown, I asked Moms to call Damon. Giving me one of her infamous *Not now* looks, Moms tried to replace it with a smile. It wasn't a good time for either of us to argue. She got Damon on the phone and gave him a status report. He made no promises. I guess he couldn't think of a quick lie, or respected Moms too much to do so.

"Aaagh!" I wailed as the pain got heavier.

I kept asking myself, *Why did I do this?*

A nurse checked me and said somethin' about two centimeters. Miss Candy and Moms listened closely, but I had no idea what the nurse meant. Glancing at the clock on the wall, I saw time was moving, but I seemed to be going nowhere. I was still carryin'. It felt like I had cramps to the tenth degree. I couldn't take the pain or the wait.

"Walk around like the nurse said. It'll make it go faster," Moms urged.

I had already strolled through the maternity ward a couple of times. Looked at the new babies. Spoken to moms-to-be like me who were cruising the halls and visiting. Walking wasn't makin' anything progress. I was already four days late. I was tired, hungry, and in horrible pain. I couldn't keep my eyes dry and didn't have the fight in me to try.

"I can't take it anymore! It hurts too much! I don't want to do this. I want to go home!" I sobbed.

Grabbing my hand, Moms rubbed it and my belly while Miss Candy tried soothing my mind.

"We know it hurts. You're doin' good. It won't be that much longer. He'll be here soon and then it'll be all over," Miss Candy explained.

Soon was no longer good enough! I needed a timeline. Exactly when would "soon" be?

While the nurse rechecked me, Moms asked her to give me somethin' for the pain. Apparently soon was still far away.

"This won't hurt. It'll just feel a little uncomfortable. No matter how uncomfortable it feels, I need you to stay absolutely still, no matter what. Okay?" some doctor with a long needle instructed me as I rolled onto my side, waiting for him to stick it into my spine.

Wow! Within several minutes, my pain was practically gone. Not all the way—I could still feel a little tightening—but it was bearable. I could manage it. Someone should have given that to me as soon as I checked in.

Miss Candy and Moms joked about my sudden change of attitude.

"I'll tell Roc he can come in now," Moms said.

"Roc? He's here?" I asked.

She explained, "Yeah, he came when I told him you were in labor. He's been waiting in the lobby. Don't laugh, but he said he didn't want to see you in pain." Then Moms left the room, bringing him back with her.

Roc looked tired, and I think "anxious" is the right word to describe the lines on his face. He patted my arm gently, like he was afraid touching me would hurt. Then he asked how I was doin'.

"Much better now that they gave me this," I said, pointing to the tube runnin' from my back to a cart.

He didn't say anything else. Slipping his hands into his pockets, Roc looked around the room. He seemed to be more uncomfortable than I had just been.

Since he wasn't talking much, Miss Candy and Moms's voices filled the air. A combination of their voices and my pain-free contractions lulled me to sleep. A light sleep, but enough shut-eye for me to refill my energy meter. Suddenly, I sprang up in pain. I then knew why it's called "labor." Having a baby is hard, back-breakin' work!

"Okay. I'm going to turn off the epidural and get the doctor. You're ready to push. If you feel the urge, go ahead and do it," the nurse ordered.

Hearing the word "push," both Roc and I got scared. He flew out of the room so fast, I thought he had wings. I wished I could have done the same.

Grabbing each hand, Moms and Miss Candy stood by my sides. I wasn't sure what urge I was supposed to be feelin'. Only thing I felt like doin' was running home and climbing into my own bed. With the doctor at my lower end and the nurse reading the monitor, I listened when they told me to push. And then I did. Well, I thought I was doin' what they told me to do, but nothin' popped out. I felt that maybe I wasn't doin' it right. I couldn't really feel anything. Suddenly I smelled somethin' awful. Quickly, the nurse changed the pads underneath me and I saw that I had crapped on the table. All I could think was, *Eeew!*

"You're doin' good, Ree Ree; keep it up."

"Yeah, c'mon, girl. You can do it," Miss Candy said.

I had been in the same position for almost forty-five minutes. On TV the woman pushes for a few minutes and then the baby pops out. I wanted the TV delivery!

"I can't do it anymore!" I cried.

The pain medication wore off and my butt felt like

it was rippin' open. I hated screaming, but I did. I hated Damon for causin' the pain I was in. I hated him more for not being there.

"Get this baby out of me!"

"Push, Ree Ree."

My vagina was burnin'. It felt hot and on fire. My mind and body were arguing with each other, the body wanting to know what the mind was thinking getting pregnant, the mind screaming back that the body did it. I wanted to get off the table and run home to bed.

"It hurts!" I hollered. "Aagh."

Moms tried to calm me. "You're doing good, baby."

"There's the head," the doctor said.

Dropping my hand, Miss Candy went and stood behind the doctor. Lookin' over his shoulder, she said, "I see the head. He has hair, too." That was more of me than I wanted to share. But I had neither the strength nor words to tell Miss Candy to get away from there.

"Okay, now push," instructed the nurse.

Holding my breath, I pushed as hard as I could, making sounds that had no meaning. The burning . . . the stretching.

"GET IT OUT OF ME!" I roared.

"Here's the head. Let me suction the nose," the doctor said. "Okay, one more push should bring this baby out."

I was exhausted. I didn't want to push anymore. I had done all the work—got fat, carried for nine months and five days, been in labor for nineteen hours, pushed for over an hour—I wondered if Damon could pick up some of the slack.

"I can't do it anymore!" I whined.

"C'mon, Ree Ree, it's almost over. Just one more push, baby."

Mustering the little bit I had left, I hollered, "UGH! I CAN'T DO IT!"

"Two seventeen a.m.," the nurse announced.

Ashy and covered with blood, *you* and some long cord were in the doctor's hands.

I was ordered to push again. I wanted to say, "What for? He's already here." But words were a waste of my strength.

"Aw, look at him," Moms said.

"He's so little," Miss Candy cooed.

While I pushed, the nurse placed you on my chest. With tears in their eyes, Moms and Miss Candy stroked your tiny patch of hair and your legs.

"Hey, little man," Moms said.

"What took you so long?" Miss Candy teased.

At that time, I couldn't bring myself to touch you. You were covered in blood and some messy yellow stuff, which looked like snot.

"Sheree, he's beautiful," Moms said.

A wave of coldness covered my body—first my knees, then my arms. My body began to shake uncontrollably. No one seemed to notice. Everyone was busy examining.

"Ten fingers, ten toes," Miss Candy said.

Moms added, "Listen to that cry, a good strong cry, too."

Cleaning.

"We'll clean him up, then she can hold him," the nurse said.

Wrapped in a tight baby blue blanket with a knit skullcap, the nurse handed me . . . but I couldn't. Moms pushed. "Here, hold him. What's his name going to be?"

"I told you, Damon Keith Parker the Second," I said.

Suckin' her teeth, Moms was now ready to tangle. "Why don't you name him something else? At least give him our last name or something."

Truly irritable, I didn't want to argue, but I could. I had to set Moms straight. "Damon Keith Parker the Second," I snapped.

Determined to get the last word, Moms said, "Well, I'm not calling him that. I'll call him D then." Still pushing, she said, "Here, hold D."

"No, you can hold him."

"No, here. You haven't held him yet."

"I know. I will."

Miss Candy brought Roc into the room.

"Here's your grandson," Moms said, offering you to Roc. He grabbed you, cradled you, like he knew how to hold a baby. "Look, he's got your chin, Roc. He was born at two seventeen, weighing six pounds even, and is seventeen inches."

Examining your chin, Roc asked, "What's today's date again?"

Answering, Miss Candy said, "February sixth."

Beaming, Roc said, "February sixth at two seventeen, six pounds, seventeen inches. I've got to play those numbers."

Conversations about how tall you would be, how dark (Moms checked your ear color), what you would be like, and who you looked like swirled around the room. Purposely, I faded into the background, never offering anything to the discussion. I was havin' my own internal dialogue. Now that you were finally here, would Damon's attitude change? Could I do this alone? Was I strong enough?

Moms asked me if she should call Damon, but I said no. I wanted to be the one to tell him and I needed to do it alone, although it didn't appear as though I was gonna get any moments to myself. Moms and Miss Candy seemed tired during my pushing. We had been at the hospital all evening and they didn't get any sleep. However, your arrival seemed to rejuvenate them. They were passing you around like a football and talkin' like they were never gonna leave your side. And seein' that you were mine, that meant my side too.

"Ree Ree hasn't held him yet. Give D to her," Moms told Miss Candy.

"That's okay. I'll have plenty of time. You can hold him, Candy," I said.

Moms was about to say somethin' else when a male nurse walked in saying he had to take you to the nursery for tests. Not used to seein' a male nurse, Roc started examining the man. When the nurse left, Roc sounded protective.

"Nowadays you can never be too sure. Whoever comes in this room, always check their ID tags. I noticed they all have a purple stripe." Roc stood up. "Look, I'd better get goin'. I'm gonna try to get some sleep before I got to be at work." He kissed my cheek. "I'll be back later and I'll bring Lil' Roc, too," Roc said.

His leaving set off a chain reaction. Miss Candy and Moms were going also. Both would be back later in the morning. Moms wanted to reclean my room, make sure it was sanitized for your arrival. As soon as they walked out of my room, I picked up the telephone and dialed Damon's cell phone.

I was surprised that he didn't answer. He knew I was at the hospital. Shouldn't he have been waiting for my call?

"Your son, Damon Keith Parker the Second, was born this morning, February sixth, at two seventeen. He weighs six pounds and is seventeen inches. Oh, and by the way, he's got your chocolate skin, and aside from his chin, looks just like you. I'm at Bryn Mawr Hospital, room three twenty-nine."

I hung up the phone and waited. Knowin' Damon, he listened to my message as soon as I hung up. I doubted he would come to the hospital right away. But I was certain—no, I was certainly hopeful—he'd visit me later in the morning.

Shutting my eyes, I tried to get some sleep. I requested that you sleep in the nursery. Who knows if you were doin' it or not. I wasn't. I couldn't. Reality—rather, fear—kept me awake. It also claimed my dry eyes.

I thought once you were here I'd feel better. Those somber feelings would escape me. Love and joy would take their place. But instead, I felt the same, if not worse: empty.

I was scared to hold you. What did I know about takin' care of babies? What if I dropped you? I was scared to give you a bottle. How would I know if you've had enough? How would I burp you? When mothers whack babies on the back, it looks so painful. I was scared to really look at you. You looked just like Damon. How was that possible? How come you didn't resemble me none? I was also scared that you would see I was scared.

Later in the morning, Moms and Miss Candy returned, bringing yellow roses. They were surprised you were still in the nursery. Immediately, Moms went to get you. Miss Candy made me eat some of the breakfast that was still on my tray. To pacify her, I took two bites of a corn muffin. I wasn't hungry.

Moms wheeled the acrylic bassinet into the room, then swooped in to pick you up. She coddled and cooed, kissed you and talked. I watched with envy; perhaps I'd learn to do that too.

Taking notice of herself, Moms said, "Look at me. Here you go." She thrust you in my face.

Putting my head down, I picked at the food on the breakfast tray.

I could feel Miss Candy and Moms eyeballin' me. Their thoughts were turnin'. Miss Candy was the first to speak. "Why don't you get a shower? You'll feel better after you get up and move around."

Finally, given a purpose, somethin' I knew how to

do, I got up and walked into the tiny bathroom. As I turned the knob, adjusting the water temperature, the bathroom seemed to get foggy. Stepping in, I let the water take me. As the water ran down my body, I looked at my stomach. It was still fat. You were here; there was no reason for me to still look pregnant. Clutching the tiny bar of soap, I couldn't remember what I was supposed to do with it. As the water got hotter and hotter, I continued staring at the soap, not usin' it at all. Suddenly remembering that I was supposed to be cleaning myself still didn't produce any action. My mind was on autopilot, but my body wasn't. I continued standing there, absorbing the heat and the water.

I must have been in the shower too long, 'cause Moms came into the bathroom. Her lips were movin', but no sound was coming out. I stared blankly, wondering why she didn't speak up. She kept movin' her lips. I kept staring, wondering why she didn't say something.

I'm not sure why, but Miss Candy came in too, cramping the little bathroom. She too was moving her lips, but to Moms not at me. I thought they were playin' a trick on me, pretending to talk. Shaking her head, Moms shut off the water, mouthed somethin', then touched my arm.

The rest of what happened was told to me much later. I try as hard as I can, but I still can't remember any of it. Moms says when she went to pull me out of the shower, I slunk down in the far corner of the stall. As she once again tried to get me to stand up, to put a pad and clothes on, I looked through her, not at her, and started giggling. Moms says I giggled like a little girl, so at first she kind of played along and laughed too. Still tryin' to get me to stand, Moms cracked what she says was a corny joke. Somethin' about the hospital food knockin' me off of my feet. Supposedly, then I fell out laughin'. Laughing. Uncontrollably. Loudly. Hysterically.

My laughter scared Miss Candy and Moms. Knowing that the joke and the situation weren't funny, Miss Candy ran to get a nurse. Feeling helpless, Moms watched in terror as my laughter metamorphosed into screaming sobs. Moms says every time she attempted to touch me, I'd recoil, balling myself into a baby position. A nurse and an orderly were able to do what Moms couldn't. They took me out of the shower, dressed me, and put me to bed. Moms says she thought I just needed some sleep. The doctor told her he believed it was deeper than that: postpartum depression.

The nurse gave me somethin' to help me sleep. I still

don't recall that part, but I do remember waking up the next day. I'd slept most of the day away. When I woke up, Moms and Roc were in the room holding you.

"Sleeping Beauty awakes," Moms joked lightly.

Ignoring the joke, I asked, "Did Damon stop by?" For some reason, Roc and Moms both looked disappointed.

As Moms shook her head, I could tell she had somethin' on her mind. But she bit her tongue. Instead, she brought you over and said, "Say hi, Mommy. I missed you."

My hands stayed by my side as I looked at your little nose, fat cheeks, and dark round face. "I'm hungry," I lied.

Moms pulled you closer and walked near the window, babbling the whole time. Roc had an uneasy look on his face. When my lunch was brought in, I didn't touch it, didn't lift the metal lid or anything. I pushed it away. My actions didn't go unnoticed, but no comments were made either. Instead, Moms left the room. Roc and I sat in silence. His attempts to make small talk were not met in kind.

Later, Moms and my doctor, Dr. Lloyd, came into the room. Dr. Lloyd asked me some questions, simple questions about how I was doin': Did I eat? Were you eating?

Wetting? Sleeping? Tears glazed my eyes as I tried to form a sentence to answer. He said something about giving me an antidepressant and my stayin' longer for observation.

I was given some pills, which allowed me to get even more sleep. The next day, I was in and out of it. Even when I was awake, I was barely talking. There was nothin' to say. Moms, Roc, Miss Candy, and the nursery staff basically took care of you. I couldn't . . . and wouldn't.

One day, I got some visitors, Ange and Austin. They were carrying flowers and wrapped gifts. Usually, seein' just one of them would bring a smile to my face. The two of them together should have brought endless joy. But I didn't feel like company, not even theirs, and my face and attitude expressed that.

"Hey, girl! Why the long face, Mommy?" Ange tried to hug me.

"Congratulations. Where's he at?" Austin asked.

My eyes came alive. "Damon? Who knows? He's probably with Ushama."

Looking shocked, Austin carefully answered, "No, the baby. We want to see the baby."

Turning my body away from them and toward the wall, I didn't answer.

Quickly, Moms stepped up, takin' them to the

nursery, I guess. They must have also gone home, because neither Ange nor Austin returned to my room. While they were gone, Roc finally revealed what was on his mind.

"I hate watching you like this. I know what Damon is doing is hurting you. Who's to say if he'll ever come around. So you can't just stop everything—eating and all—waiting. D needs you. He needs his mom, not his grandmom."

Still facing the wall, I quietly asked, "But why? Why is Damon doing this? Why did you do it?"

I knew my question would put Roc on the spot. And at that point, I didn't care. In all these years, we had never talked about why he did the things he did. Over that time, I just accepted his ways as just that, but I'd be lyin' if I didn't admit that I always wanted to know why. Why didn't he act like a daddy?

Roc didn't answer right away. After a few minutes, I turned around to face him. He looked exactly like how I was feelin' inside. Rubbing his chin, perhaps searching for an answer, Roc finally spoke.

"I didn't know how to be a dad, a real dad. My pops was never around. Sometimes he'd pop up late and drunk on Christmas Eve, give my mom some money, speak to me, and roll out. Eventually, I did more than that, so I thought I was two steps better than him."

Correcting him, I interrupted. "No, Moms says you weren't around when I was born."

Roc met my eyes. "No. I wasn't. I missed all of y'all being born except Lil' Roc. When you, Eric, and Randy were born, I was still young. Still hangin' in the streets bein' cool. I wasn't ready to be a dad or get a nine-to-five. I was doin' thangs my way, and no woman, no matter how fine she was, was gonna make me stop hustlin' and start being responsible. That's what your moms wanted. Stacey wanted me to get a job so the three of us could get an apartment and then get married. When I first met your moms, I saw that fantasy in her eyes. I'm ashamed to tell you now because I'm not like that no more, but I'm gonna tell you because I have a feeling Damon played on your same fantasy weakness. Since your moms wanted somebody to take care of her because her dad didn't, I used that to my advantage. I acted like I'd always be there; gave her money, made her think she was at the top of my list as far as women were concerned. But when she got pregnant, I froze and got scared.

"Damon saw that I wasn't really part of your life and he tried to play daddy with you, too. It's the same game, just different playas. Now that you changed the game, by adding D to the mix, Damon is probably scared too. He knows the streets; he knows women; he knows runnin' drugs; but he doesn't know how to be a daddy. Ain't no cats hangin' on the corners talking about buyin' diapers or spending time with their kids or baby's mama. No, as I look at it now, all our talk is about avoidance. 'Yo, man, if this one acts up, I'm'a kick it with her'—that's how we do.

"I thought that was how men did it. Couldn't nobody have told me then, but I wasn't a man." Roc paused. "And now today, I'm still learning. I'm really workin' on it."

I had to ask, "Did you love me?"

Without hesitation, Roc said, "Yeah, of course I loved you. I love you now, too. Back then, I just didn't know how to love you, do for you. I was still out there, so I had to let your mom raise you, but I see now how you needed me, too. I didn't know that. I thought girls just need their mamas. But now I see what happens if their daddies ain't in the picture; other boys claimin' to be men take on the role and they become users like I was. And don't get me wrong, boys need strong daddies too. I think Lil' Roc's got that. I'm tryin' now to give it to Eric and Randy, 'cause they missed out too."

"Roc, what can I do to make Damon see that his son needs him?"

Roc gave me a heartbreaking look and answered,

"Nothing. There's nothing you can do. He has to see it on his own. Your mom tried to show me and it backfired. The more she tried demanding things and leanin' on me, the more I pulled away. It's a rebellious attitude. You got to let Damon go, take him to court for child support, and then go on and raise D and forget about Damon. Why make someone see their child? Forcing Damon won't make him be the dad you want him to be.

"Look at us. This is the first time I've ever sat down and really talked with you. I missed out on so much. Your birth, milestones, stuff like that, I missed because I was being cool in the streets. As I look at D and Lil' Roc, I feel like God is giving me another chance to do this thing right. I messed up! Messed up, big-time! I wasn't a dad to you and I'm tryin to make up for all that lost time now."

Since I had returned from Milagro House, Roc had been comin' around more. But I was still doubtful that he had changed for good, so I looked at him deeply with skepticism and with hope. He understood my message.

"I know; you don't have to say it. Yeah, I'm for real this time. I didn't just watch Dr. Phil or go to church. Sheree, when you ran away, Stacey came and showed me your letter. It took a while for me to process all that was written. But I saw how I had caused some of the troubles you were feeling. I never knew about Kevin. I wasn't your bridge. I wasn't there for you when you needed me and I'm never again going to be that caught up with myself that my own child can't talk to me or ask me for anything. When I look at you having a baby, so young, like your mom and I did, I see you cryin' for attention. I see that I did it all wrong. But that was the past and I'm movin' forward, making changes."

Roc's eyes met my own waterfall. Rushing to my side, he hugged me tightly, telling me everything would be okay.

Those were the last tears I shed over Damon. I cried my past away, dried my eyes toward my future. If Roc could make some changes, so could I—starting with your name. Yes, for the first few days of your life you were called Damon by me, D by Moms and Roc. After my conversation with Roc, I realized Moms was right, Damon didn't deserve such a special honor. He would always be your dad. It was up to him whether he would act like one or not. So I renamed you Beauford Dianthus Jemison. Quite a mouthful, so we just call you Bee.

Beauford is actually Roc's real name, although few people know that. Dianthus, or D for short, is one of Mom's favorite flowers. It grows every summer in Moms's and Mom Mom's gardens. Look for the pretty-smelling white and pink flowers.

Unfortunately, as of this date, August 2005, Damon still isn't a part of your life. (When he is, I'll write another letter.) He has seen you, though. Once, when I took you in your stroller up to the courts, he worked his way over and looked down at your handsome chocolate face. There was no denying that you were his, but he hasn't stepped up yet. Yes, that hurt and it still does. But I figure Roc's right; it's Damon's loss. You are beautiful; he's the fool for missin' out.

My life no longer revolves around Damon or any other man's needs. Well, one man—one man-to-be. That's *you*. Everything I do is about you right now.

I didn't know anything about havin' a baby, especially a boy, but I'm learning. Still learning. I am determined that you are gonna be a good man. One who knows how to treat his mother, women, and children. I'm going to see to that, and so is Roc, your g-pop.

On June 6, Moms got her wish. I crossed the threshold, turning my tassel, graduating from high school. In September, Roc's wish will come true. He's helping me to become a certified gardener. I'll be taking courses at Longwood Gardens. With any luck, I'll eventually get a job there. Given our family's history, landscaping makes sense. But even with everything I already know about flowers and houseplants, I still have so much more to learn. So I'll be studying about different types of soil, trees and shrubs, and design.

And my wish? Well, in a way, the love I was searchin' for back at the beginning of last summer still eludes me. Once again, I'm on a one-way street. Babies don't give love, they take. They take, quite simply, because they need. You take up all of my time, my little bit of money, my sleep, my freedom, my patience, and my love. And that's okay. I finally got it. It's not about me no more. It's all about you. So don't get me wrong, I love you to death. We had a rough start, but we're on our way. You have made me a better person, a stronger person. One who isn't out partyin', chasing guys no more. I needed to change, because before, I was slowly dying. I want you to learn from my mistakes, because I made a lot of 'em. One day, when you're old enough to read and understand this letter, we'll talk about some of them. If I had known back when I was younger what I know now, I would have worked on loving Sheree more. You would have been created in my future, after I knew and loved, really loved, *myself* first.

Much love, my sweet little man,

Mommy

AUTHOR'S NOTE

Although the characters and events in Baby Girl are a work of my imagination, one place is real: Milagro House. Milagro House is a transitional home for women and their children in Lancaster, Pennsylvania.

In the fall of 2001 I became a volunteer at Milagro House. I met people there from all walks of life. Some women's stories are similar to Sheree's and Ange's, and some are far worse. But as long as those women have a desire to change, Milagro House is a great safety net.

The nonprofit agency isn't a temporary shelter and doesn't offer a quick fix. Milagro House offers long-term housing where counseling, career training, and parental classes are mandatory. Once women have the skills, the staff and its supporters at Milagro House help these women and their children find permanent housing. In some cases permanent housing has meant home ownership.

While the work done at Milagro House is a work of love for the founder and director, Renee Valentine, it doesn't come cheap. The nonprofit organization is always in need of funds and volunteers.

If you are in a difficult situation and need help, please check your local yellow pages or the Internet for an agency to help you.